WEDDING DATE WITH THE ARMY DOC

BY
LYNNE MARSHALL

MILLS & BOON

First published in Great Britain 2016
By Mills & Boon, an imprint of HarperCollins*Publishers*
1 London Bridge Street, London, SE1 9GF

Large Print edition 2017

© 2016 Janet Maarschalk

ISBN: 978-0-263-06674-6

Our policy is to use papers that are natural, renewable and recyclable products and made from wood grown in sustainable forests. The logging and manufacturing processes conform to the legal environmental regulations of the country of origin.

Printed and bound in Great Britain
by CPI Antony Rowe, Chippenham, Wiltshire

Summer Brides

Two unexpected journeys to 'I do'—
two perfect summer weddings...

Stunning Ashley Marsh and beautiful doctor
Charlotte Johnson have vowed never to risk
it all for love—but the hotshot docs they
work with are an irresistible temptation!

ER doc Kiefer Bradford and army doc
Jackson Hilstead are hotter than the summer
sun, and before they know it these two
guarded heroines find their vows undone...

Now they must find the courage
to make the most important vows of all.
And what could be more romantic than
not one but *two* summer weddings?

Find out what happens in:

White Wedding for a Southern Belle
by Susan Carlisle

Wedding Date with the Army Doc
by Lynne Marshall

Summer Brides

Available now!

Dear Reader,

A few years ago I thought up a story about a female pathologist and ran it by my editor. The story had many flaws and needed much work. At the time I opted to put it away in a drawer, but I didn't stop thinking about it. After letting the story rest for a while I went back to it and, with the extensive notes I'd received from my editor the first time around, I reworked everything. I'm so happy I did.

Charlotte, my courageous pathologist, made a life-changing decision based on a potential killer that many women have to face. Cancer. She opted to be pre-emptive, and her decision was radical, but in her mind it was saving her life. She had strong reasons for making this decision, based on watching her mother's battle with and eventual defeat by cancer.

Jackson had everything going for him in life until a second tour of Afghanistan on an army medical team changed everything. He came home wounded and lost, and the already weakened fabric of his marriage didn't hold up under the stress. But, having almost lost it all, he courageously fought his way back and changed direction. Unfortunately divorce was part of that change, but a new beginning three thousand miles across country in California turned out to be his saving grace.

Picture a small pathology office in the basement of a hospital, where these two wounded and healing people come together in a most unromantic way. Against all odds love still raises its head, as well as the consciousness of these two meant-to-be people. All it takes is their willingness to risk another chance at love.

Is it worth it? Come read Charlotte and Jackson's story, so you can make your own decision.

Lynne

lynnemarshall.com

'Friend' me on Facebook!

Lynne Marshall used to worry that she had a serious problem with daydreaming—and then she discovered she was supposed to *write* those stories! A Registered Nurse for twenty-six years, she came to fiction writing later than most. Now she writes romance which usually includes medicine but always comes straight from her heart. She is happily married, a Southern California native, a woman of faith, a dog-lover, an avid reader, a curious traveller and a proud grandma.

Books by Lynne Marshall

Mills & Boon Medical Romance

The Hollywood Hills Clinic
His Pregnant Sleeping Beauty

Cowboys, Doctors...Daddies!
Hot-Shot Doc, Secret Dad
Father For Her Newborn Baby

Temporary Doctor, Surprise Father
The Boss and Nurse Albright
The Heart Doctor and the Baby
The Christmas Baby Bump
Dr Tall, Dark...and Dangerous?
NYC Angels: Making the Surgeon Smile
200 Harley Street: American Surgeon in London
A Mother for His Adopted Son

Visit the Author Profile page
at millsandboon.co.uk for more titles.

Many thanks to Flo Nicoll,
with her uncanny gift of pinpointing the
missing link in my manuscripts and for
giving me the freedom to explore diverse
and difficult stories.

Also, I'd like to dedicate this book to the
'Dr Gordon' I remember so well from my
first job, working in a pathology department.
I learned so much and was given
many opportunities all those years ago!
Knowing 'Dr Gordon' changed the
direction of my life. May he rest in peace.

**Praise for
Lynne Marshall**

'Heartfelt emotion that will bring you
to the point of tears, for those who love
a second-chance romance written with
exquisite detail.'
—*Contemporary Romance Reviews* on
NYC Angels: Making the Surgeon Smile

'Lynne Marshall contributes a rewarding
story to the *NYC Angels* series, and her
gifted talent repeatedly shines. *Making the
Surgeon Smile* is an outstanding romance
with genuine emotions and passionate
desires.'
—*CataRomance*

CHAPTER ONE

CHARLOTTE JOHNSON MADE the necessary faces to chew the amazing chocolate, nut and caramel candy she'd just shoved into her mouth between looking at pathology slides. Mid-nut-and-caramel-chew, she glanced up to see a hulking shadow cover her office door. Her secret surgeon crush, Jackson Ryland Hilstead the Third, blocked the fluorescent light from the hallway, causing her to narrow her eyes in order to make out his features. *Be still, my heart, and, oh, heavens, stop chewing. Now!*

Except she couldn't talk unless she finished chewing and swallowed, and she figured he'd come for a reason, as he always did Friday afternoons. Probably because of his heavy schedule of surgeries on Thursday and Friday mornings. He'd ask her questions about his patients' diagnoses and prognoses, and she'd dutifully answer. It had become their routine, and she looked forward to it. After all, as the staff surgical pathologist at St. Francis of the Valley Hospital, it was her job to be helpful to her fellow medical colleagues, even while, in his case, thinking how she'd love to brush that one brown, wavy lock of hair off his forehead. Yeah, she was hopelessly crushing on the man.

She lifted her finger, hoping her sign for "One moment" might compute with the astute doc, then covered her mouth with the other hand as she chewed furiously. Finally, she swallowed with a gulp, feeling heat rise from her neck upward. *Great impression.*

"Don't let me interfere," he said, an amused look on his face. "The last thing I want to do is come between a woman and her chocolate." Obviously he'd noticed the candy-bar wrapper on her desk.

She grabbed a bottle of water and took a quick swig. "You're sounding sexist. How unlike you," she teased, hoping she didn't have candy residue on her teeth. Of all the male doctors she dealt with on a daily basis, this surgeon was the one who made her feel self-conscious. It most certainly had a lot to do with his piercing blue eyes that the hospital scrubs seemed to highlight brighter than an OR lamp. She pulled her lab coat closed when his eyes surreptitiously and briefly scanned her from head to toe. Or as much as he could see of her with her sitting behind her double-headed microscope.

"Ah, Charlotte…" He sat down across from her. "How well you *don't* know me. If you weren't my favorite pathologist, I'd be offended." Finally responding to her halfhearted "sexist" slur.

The guy was a Southern gentleman from Georgia, and she wasn't above stereotyping him, because he was a walking billboard for good manners, charm and—perhaps not quite as appealing considering the odds in a competitive and overstocked female world, in California anyway—knowing how to relate to women. The word *smooth* came to mind. But it was balanced with sincerity, a rare combination. Plus there was no escaping that slow, rolling-syllable accent, like warm honey down her spine, setting off all sorts of nerve endings she'd otherwise forgotten. He spoke as though they had all the time in the world to talk. She could listen to him all day, and if she'd owned a fan she'd be flapping it now.

"Well, if you weren't *one* of my favorite surgeons," she lied, as he was her absolute favorite, "I would've eaten the rest of it."

One corner of his mouth hitched the tiniest bit. "I think you already have, but don't worry, your gooey-chocolate choice would be number ten on my list of top three favorite candy bars."

Busted, she batted her lashes, noticing his spearmint-and-sandalwood scent as he moved closer. She inhaled a little deeper, thinking he liked to change up his aftershave, and that intrigued her.

"And since you brought up the subject of sexism, I've got to say you look great today. Turquoise suits you."

He regularly paid her compliments, which she loved, but figured he was like that with all the women he encountered, so she never took them too seriously. Though she had to admit she longed for him to mean them. What did that say about her dating life? Something in the way his eyes watched her and waited for a response whenever he flattered her made her wonder if maybe she was a tiny bit more special than all the other ladies in the hospital. She liked the idea of that.

"Thank you," she said, sounding as self-effacing as ever.

"Thank *you*," he countered.

Their gazes held perhaps a second longer than she could take, so she pretended the slide on the microscope tray required her immediate and complete attention. "So what do you need?"

Intensely aware of his *do-you-really-want-to-know?* gaze—this was new and it was a challenge that shook her to the bone—she fought the urge to squirm. Yeah, sexist or sexy or whatever it was he just did with those eyes was way out of her comfort zone. So why did that look excite her, make her wish things could be the way they had been before her operation? Where was that invisible fan again? Shame. Shame. Shame. And she called herself a professional woman.

"Do you have the slides yet for Gary Underwood? A lung biopsy from yesterday afternoon.

I've got an impatient wife demanding her husband's results."

"The weekend is coming, so I can understand her concern." Charlotte hadn't yet finished the slides from yesterday morning's cases, but she was always willing to fish out a few newer ones for interested doctors. Jackson was as concerned about his patients as they came. Another thing she really liked about the guy.

She turned on the desk lamp, sorted through the pile of cardboard slide cases, each carefully labeled by the histology technicians, and found the slides in question. They settled in to study them, their knees nearly touching as they sat on opposite sides of the small table that held her dual-headed teaching microscope. She put her hair behind her ears and moved in, but not before seeing him notice her dangly turquoise earrings that matched her top. She could tell from the spark in his eyes that he liked them, too, but this time kept the fact to himself.

Yes, he was a real gentleman, with broad shoulders and wavy brown hair that he chose to comb straight back from his forehead. And it was just long enough to curl under his ears. Call him a sexy gentleman. *Gulp.* Very, very sexy.

Being smack in the heart of the San Fernando Valley was nothing new for an original Valley girl like her, but she figured it had to be total culture shock for a man from Savannah. *Talk to me, baby. I love that Southern drawl.* Why did she have such confidence inside her head but could never dare to act on it? She didn't waste a single second answering that question. Because things were different now. She wasn't the woman she'd used to be. Enough said.

In his early forties with a sprinkling of gray at his temples, Jackson had only been in Southern California for a year. Word was, if she could believe everything she heard from Dr. Dupree, Jackson had needed a change after his divorce. Which made him a gentleman misfit in a casual-with-a-capital-C kind of town. She liked that about him, too—the khaki slacks and button-down collared shirts with ties that he'd obviously given some time to selecting. Today the shirt was pale yellow and the tie an expensive-looking subtly sage-green herringbone pattern. Nice.

She turned off the desk light so they could view the slide better. They sat in companionable silence as they studied it. Hearing him breathe ever so gently made the hair on the back of her neck stand on end. Good thing she'd worn it down today. Hmm, maybe that was what he liked? *Stop it, Charlotte. This will never go anywhere.* Maybe that was why she enjoyed the fantasy so much. It was her secret. And it was safe.

She fine-focused on the biopsied lung tissue, increasing the magnification over one particular spot of red-dyed swirls with minuscule black dots until the cells came into full view. They studied the areas in question together. "Notice the angulated nuclear margins and hyperchromasia in this area?" She spoke close to a whisper, a habit she'd got into out of respect for the solemn importance of each patient's diagnosis.

"Hmm," he emitted thoughtfully.

She moved the slide on the tray a tiny bit, then refocused. "And here, and here." She used the white teaching arrow in the high-grade microscope to point out the areas in question.

He inhaled, his eyes never leaving the eyepiece.

"Here are mitotic figures, and here intercellular bridges. Not a good sign." She pulled back from her microscope. "As you can see, there are variations in size of cells and nuclei, which adds up to squamous cell malignancy. I'll have to study the rest of the slides to check the margins and figure out the cancer staging, but, unfortunately, the anxiously awaiting wife will have more to be anxious about."

"Bad news for sure." Jackson pushed back from the microscope, but not before one of his knees knocked hers, and it hurt her kneecap, feeling almost like metal. Maybe he was Superman in disguise? "I'll get in touch with Oncology to get a jump on things."

The situation caused an old and familiar pang in her stomach. Charlotte knew how it felt to be a family member waiting for news from the doctor. She'd gone through the process at fifteen, the year her mother had been diagnosed with breast cancer. That was the day she'd first heard the term *metastatic* and had vowed to figure out what it meant. And after that she'd vowed to learn everything she could about her mother's condition.

"Is he young and otherwise healthy?"

"Yes," Jackson said. "Which will help the prognosis."

She nodded, though not enthusiastically. Her mother had been young and supposedly healthy, too. The loss of her mother soon after bilateral mastectomies had broken her family's heart. Her father had never recovered, and within a span of three years of his downhill slide, he'd also died. From alcoholism, his self-medication of choice to deal with the emotional pain. She'd already stepped in as the responsible one when her mother had first been diagnosed, and after she'd died Charlotte had kept the family functioning. Barely. At eighteen, along with applying to colleges, she'd signed on to be the guardian of her kid sister and brother, otherwise they'd have ended up in foster homes.

Her mother's cancer had changed the course of her life, steering her toward medicine, and later, with her never-ending quest to understand why things happened as they did, sending her into the darker side of the profession, pathology.

"Well, I've got to run," Jackson said, bringing her out of her thoughts. "I've got a dinner I can't miss tonight, and Mrs. Underwood to talk to first." He stood and took a couple of steps then turned at her office door and looked at her again thoughtfully. "Do you happen to know off-hand the extension for social services? I think the Underwoods could use some added support this weekend."

Having put the desk light back on, she scanned her hospital phone list cheat sheet and read out the numbers, admittedly disappointed to know he had a dinner engagement.

"Thanks," he said, but not before giving her a thorough once-over again. "Really like those earrings, too." Then he left, leaving her grinning with warming cheeks.

Wanting desperately to read more into his light flattery than she should, she groaned quietly. The guy had a dinner date! Plus the man probably said things like that to all the women he encountered in his busy days. It had probably been drilled into him back in Georgia since grade school, maybe even before that. Treat all women like princesses.

Who was she kidding, hoping she might be

more special than other women he knew? She was five feet nine, a full-figured gal, or had used to be anyway, a size ten, and not many men appreciated that in this thin-as-a-rail era. Besides, even if he did find her attractive, nothing could ever come of it. She'd pretty much taken care of that two years ago with her surgery.

Odds were most men wouldn't want to get involved with her. She pulled her lab coat tighter across her chest. Her ex-boyfriend had sure changed his mind, calling off their short engagement. They'd been all set to go the conventional route, and she'd loved the idea of having a career, marriage and kids. Her mouth had watered for it. Then...

She'd cut Derek some slack, though, since her decision had been extreme and radical even. They'd talked about it over and over, argued, and he'd never really signed on. He hadn't wanted to go there. He'd wanted her exactly as she had been.

The memory of her mother suffering had been the major influence on her final decision.

Her hand came to rest on her chest. The realistic-feeling silicone breast forms—otherwise known as falsies—she wore in her bra sometimes nearly made her forget she'd had a double mastectomy. Elective surgery.

She fiddled with Mr. Underwood's slides, lining them up to study them more thoroughly.

She'd accidentally found her own damn cancer marker right here in her office. Along with the excitement and anticipation of getting engaged and the plans for having a family, some deeper, sadder dialogue threaded through the recesses of her brain. One morning she'd woken in a near panic. What if? She'd shivered over the potential answer. Then, unable to move forward with a gigantic question mark in her future, she'd had the lab draw her blood and do the genetic marker panel. The results had literally made her gasp and grab her chest. Her worst nightmare was alive and living in her DNA.

Knowing her mother's history, the near torture she'd gone through, well, having preemptive surgery had been a decision she'd known she'd have to make. Why not take care of it before it ever had a chance to begin? She'd begged Derek to understand. He'd fought her decision, but he'd never seen what her mother had gone through.

Jackson appeared at her door again, making her lose her train of thought. He inclined his head. "You okay?"

"Oh, yes." She recovered quickly, and he obviously accepted her answer since the concern dissolved from his face.

"Hey, I forgot to ask just now. Are you going to that garden party Sunday afternoon?"

Her old concerns suddenly forgotten, the hair on her arms joined the hair on the back of her neck in prickling. Was it possible that the handsome Southern doctor was actually interested in her?

"Yes. I kind of thought it was mandatory." It was July, the newest residents would all be there and it was a chance to put names to faces.

"Good. I'll see you there, then." And off he went again, his long legs and unusual gait taking that Southern stroll to a new level.

For an instant she let her hopes take flight. What would it be like to date again, especially with a man's man like Jackson Hilstead the

Third? But he'd made no offer to go to the garden party together, and after all the thoughts she'd had just now, she wasn't a bit closer to making her secret crush real. No way.

Feeling the fallout from rehashing her past, she exchanged the instantaneous hope for reality. There was no way anyone would want her. Not with the anything-but-sexy scars across her nearly flat chest.

She sat staring into her lap, letting the truth filter through her.

Dr. Antwan Dupree appeared at her door, a man so full of himself she wished she could post a "closed for business" sign and pretend no one was home.

"I brought you some Caribbean food from a little place nearby. Thought you might like to try a taste of your heritage."

"I'm not from the Caribbean."

"Yes, you are. You just don't know it. Look at your honey-colored skin and the loads of wavy, almost black hair. Darlin', you've got Caribbean brown eyes. There's no question."

"It's brown. My hair is dark brown. Both my

parents were from the States. My grandparents were from the States. My great-grandparents were from the States. I'm typical Heinz Fifty-Seven American. The name Johnson is as American as it gets."

"I see the islands in you."

"And that makes it so? Must be nice to live in your world." She suppressed a sigh. She always had to try her best not to be rude to the young, overconfident surgeon, because she did have to work with him.

"I'm just trying to help you get in touch with your roots. Try this. It's rice and peas and jerk chicken. You'll love it."

"I don't do spicy." She opened the brown bag, pulled out the take-out container and peered inside. Black-eyed peas were something she'd never tried before, but the rice was brown, the chicken looked juicy and, since the doctor had gone to the trouble to bring the food, she figured she should at least taste it. "But I'll give this a try."

"When you eat that you'll be singing, 'I'm home, at last!'" He had an okay voice, but she wasn't ready for a serenade right then.

"I doubt it, but thanks for the thought." Her number one thought, while staring at her unrequested lunch, was how to get rid of Antwan Dupree.

Just as Antwan opened his mouth to speak again Jackson appeared once more at the door, which pleased her to no end.

Would you look at me, the popular pathologist? The thought nearly made her spew a laugh, but that could get messy and spread germs and it definitely wouldn't be attractive and Jackson was standing right there. She kept her near guffaw to herself and secretly reveled in the moment, though inwardly she rolled her eyes at the absurdity of the notion. Popular pathologist. Right.

Antwan was a pest. Jackson Hilstead, well, was not!

"Give it a try, let me know what you think." Antwan turned for the door. "You have my number, right?" He made a point to look directly at Jackson when he said that.

"Thank you and good-bye." She'd never found swagger appealing. She'd also learned that with Antwan it was best to be blunt, otherwise the guy imagined all kinds of improbable things. The thing that really didn't make sense was that he was better than decent looking and had loads of women interested around the hospital. Why pester her?

He nodded. "We'll talk later," he promised confidently, and did his unique Antwan Dupree walk right past Jackson, who hadn't budged from his half of the entrance.

"Doctor." Jackson tipped his head.

"Doctor." Dupree paid the same respect on his way out. No sooner had he left than Charlotte could hear Antwan chatting up Latoya, the receptionist down the hall. What a guy.

"Sorry to interrupt," Jackson said.

"Not at all. In fact, thank you!"

Jackson smiled and her previously claustrophobic office, with Dr. Dupree inside plus him now being gone, seemed to expand toward the universe.

"Spicy beans and rice give me indigestion, but I guess I have to try this now. I was actually kind of looking forward to my peanut butter and jelly sandwich."

That got another smile from him, and she longed to think of a thousand ways to keep them coming. She also felt compelled to clarify a few things. "For the record," she said as she closed the food container and put it back in the bag, "there is nothing at all going on between me and Dupree. He, well…he's a player and I really don't care for men who are full of themselves, you know?"

"He does like the ladies." Jackson hadn't budged from his spot at the door, and she began to wonder why he'd made another visit. "But in this case he does exhibit excellent taste."

Really? He thought she was attractive? Before she let herself get all puffed up about his comment, it occurred to her that Jackson must have come back to her office for a reason. Maybe he wanted to ask her to go with him to the garden party? "Did you need something?"

"Yes."

She mentally crossed her fingers.

"I was just talking to Dr. Gordon. He said he'd like to speak to you when you have a chance."

The head of pathology, Dr. Gordon, was her personal mentor, and admittedly a kind of father figure, and when he called, she never hesitated. "Oh. Sure, thanks." She stood and walked around her desk, then noticed the subtle gaze again from Jackson covering her from head to toe. If only she hadn't chosen sensible shoes today! But she thanked the manufacturer of realistic-looking falsies for filling out her special mastectomy bra underneath her turquoise top.

Charlotte strolled side by side with the tall doctor down the hall. She pegged him to be around six-two, based on her five-nine and wearing low wedge shoes, plus the fact her eyes were in line with his classic long and straight nose, except for that small bump on the bridge that gave him such character. She forced her attention away from his face, again noticing his subtly unusual gait, like maybe one shoe didn't fit quite right. When they reached Dr. Gordon's office door, she faked casual and said good-bye.

When he smiled his good-bye, she secretly sighed—what was it about that guy?—and lingered, watching him leave the department.

"You coming in or are you going to stand out there gawking all afternoon?" As head of pathology, Dr. Gordon had taken her under his wing from her very first day as a resident at St. Francis, and she owed him more than she could ever repay. She also happened to adore the nearly seventy-year-old curmudgeon, with his shocking white hair and clear hazel eyes that had always seemed to see right through her. His double chin helped balance a hawk-like nose.

"Sorry. Hi." She stepped inside his office. "You wanted to talk to me?"

He grew serious. "Close the door."

His instruction sent a chill through her core. Something important was about to happen and the thought made her uncomfortable. He'd better not be retiring because she wasn't ready for him to leave! She did what she was told, closed the door, then sat across from him at the desk, hoping she wasn't about to get reprimanded for something.

He gave his fatherly smile, and immediately she knew she had nothing to worry about. "I'm not going to mince words. My prostate cancer is back and Dr. Hilstead is going to do exploratory surgery on me Monday. I want you to read the frozen sections."

Stunned, she could hardly make herself speak. "Yes. Of course." She wanted to run to him and throw her arms around him, but they didn't have that kind of relationship. "Whatever you want." His wife, Elly, had passed away last year, and he'd seemed so forlorn ever since. The last thing the man needed was a cancer threat. Her heart ached for him, but she fought to hide her fears. "I'll go over those specimens with a fine-tooth comb."

"And I'll expect no less." Stoic as always. Pathology had a way of doing that to doctors.

"Is there anything I can do for you this weekend?"

"Thank you but no. My son is flying in from Arizona for a few days."

"I'm glad to hear that."

"Oh, wait, there is something you could do. I guess you could fill in for me on Sunday afternoon at that new resident garden party deal."

"Of course." Not her favorite idea, since she'd hoped she could find a way to comfort him, like make a big pot of healthy soup or something, but she'd planned to go to the Sunday event anyway.

The good doctor winked at her. "Whatever we find, we'll nip it in the bud, right?"

"You bet." With her heart aching, she wished she could guarantee that would be the case, but they passed a look between them that said it all. As pathologists, they knew when cancer reared its head the hunt was on. It was their job to be relentless in tracking it down, the surgeons' job to cut it out, and the oncologists' to find the magic healing potion to obliterate anything that was left.

Medical science was a tough business, and Charlotte Johnson had signed on in one of the most demanding fields. Pathology. She'd never get used to being the bearer of bad news. Usually the doctors had to take it from there once she handed over the medical verdict. She considered Jim Gordon to be a dear friend as well as colleague and any findings she came up with he'd know had come directly from her. The responsibility unsettled her stomach.

Now that she'd dealt with her own deepest

fear—and Jim Gordon had condoned her radical decision two years ago at the age of thirty-two—she was damned if she'd give up being an optimist for him.

Come Monday morning she'd be ready for the toughest call of her career, and it would be for Dr. Gordon. Her mentor. The man she'd come to respect like a father. But first she'd have to make it through the garden party on Sunday afternoon, and the one bright spot in that obligation was the chance to see her secret surgeon crush again. Dr. Jackson Hilstead.

CHAPTER TWO

CHARLOTTE DIDN'T WANT to admit she'd picked the Capri blue patterned sundress only because Dr. Hilstead had liked her turquoise top on Friday, though the thought had entered her mind while searching her closet for something to wear on Sunday morning.

It had been a long time since she'd even considered wearing a dress cut like this, which made her feel uncomfortable, so she'd compromised with a white, lightweight, very loosely knit, three-quarter-sleeved summer sweater. To help cover the dipping neckline, she chose several strings of large and colorful beads. On a whim, she left her hair down, letting the thick waves touch the tops of her shoulders and making no excuses for the occasional ringlet around her face. And this shade of blue sure made her caramel-colored eyes stand out.

With confidence, later that afternoon, she stepped into the St. Francis of the Valley atrium, which connected to an outdoor patio where dozens of doctors had already begun to gather. At the moment she didn't recognize a single face, all of the residents looking so young and eager. But there was Antwan with a young and very attractive woman on his arm. Relieved he wasn't alone, she glanced around the cavernous room.

She recognized several large painted canvases and they drew her attention to the bright white walls as she realized the ocularist down the hall from her office, Andrea Rimmer, had painted them. In fact, she'd bought several of her early paintings at an art auction because she'd loved her style so much, but these paintings were signed with a different name because Andrea had married a pediatrician, Sam Marcus, so her name had changed now. Anyway, the paintings of huge eyes peeking through various openings were amazing, each iris completely different from the next, and Charlotte was soon swept up in imagining their meaning.

Totally engrossed with admiring the newest paintings of her current favorite artist, she jumped when someone tapped her shoulder. That flutter of excitement flitted right on by when she realized it was Dr. Dupree.

"You're looking extra fine today," he said, making a show of looking her up and down.

"Thank you. Where's your date?"

"Getting some refreshments." His line of vision stayed on her chest. "All those necklaces remind me of the Caribbean."

"They're just some beads I threw on, that's all. Oh, look." She really wanted to divert his interest from her chest. "Your lady friend is searching for you."

"If I didn't assume you'd have a date today, I would have asked you myself."

"I'm here as the representative of the pathology department. This garden party is all business for me."

"Such a shame. If you ever want to actually have a good time, let me know. You don't know what you're missing until you've gone out with me."

Seriously? "If this is any example of how you

treat your dates, count me out. Now go spend some time with the very attractive woman you've brought. Shoo." She used her hands to shoo him away, like the pest he was. Man, it ticked her off how he treated women as interchangeable objects.

Frustration and anger interfered with her enjoying the artwork, and though she already really wanted to leave, she had promised Dr. Gordon to be the face of Pathology today. So she forced herself to head toward the refreshment table, where several of the new doctors stood talking among themselves. She glanced up in time to see something to make her get excited. Jackson Hilstead was easy to spot, being a head taller than others in his group, as he moved into the atrium. Charlotte found her smile come to a halt when she noticed that to Jackson's right was the assistant head of the hospital laboratory, Yuri Ito. His hand rested on her shoulder, like he was guiding her. Obviously they'd come together.

Why had Jackson asked if she was coming to the party if he was bringing a date? Her previous excitement turned to disappointment, making the thought of eating sour on her tongue. What else was new? Why had she even let herself follow her fancy in the first place? Antwan may have been right about the surgeon. Maybe he was as much of a lady's man as Dupree. What was up with surgeons?

Halfheartedly, she moved on to the buffet and picked a few items to pretend she was busy, rather than try to make eye contact with Jackson. What was the point? She greeted a few of the new residents, introducing herself and inviting them to stop by anytime for a quick tour of the department. The two young women and one guy all seemed very receptive, maybe even a little too enthusiastic. The dip may have looked great but it tasted bland, matching her mood, since eyeing the tall surgeon with Yuri, but she forced herself to partake.

Another tap on the shoulder sent her heart skittering once more, until she turned to face Antwan again. How did he keep ditching his date?

"Here," he said, handing her a glass of punch. "You'll like this—it's for grown-ups. And it reminds me—"

"Let me guess—of the Caribbean? Evidently everything does today." She took the drink and sipped, pleasantly surprised by the sweet taste with a kick, as it was definitely a grown-up beverage. "Thanks." She forced a smile and received a much-too-eager grin in return. The sight made her eyes immediately dance away in time to connect with Jackson's where he stood a few feet away.

"Hi," he said, over the crowd.

"Hello," she mouthed back.

Jackson couldn't miss Antwan standing right beside her, which was probably why he quickly looked away. But she'd been clear with him about having nothing going on with Dr. Dupree, and hoped he'd believed her. Which further proved that looks could be deceiving.

So much for getting all dolled up for a man. Except Antwan seemed to appreciate her efforts. Backfire! "Oh, look, there's your date. Isn't she one of the new surgical residents? I'm going to introduce myself."

Antwan's smile faded quickly, and that brought hers back to life as she made her way over to the pretty African-American doctor across the room.

She particularly enjoyed watching the too-sure-of-himself doctor squirm.

As the afternoon wore on and she got to know a few of the new batch of residents, who'd just begun working at the hospital July first, she secretly kept tabs on Jackson, who never left Yuri's side, though it sure didn't seem like they had much to say to each other. As in her case with Antwan, could looks be deceiving there, too?

Don't get your hopes up. She felt the urge to adjust her specially made bra but fought it. *This further proves the uselessness of secret crushes. Oh, they're fine when you keep them secret, but start letting them out on a rope and disasters like this happened.* Reality was like looking into a magnifying mirror. *What I see up close is never pleasant.*

She glanced up to find Jackson watching her, and, as crazy as her thoughts had been seconds before, that mere eye contact from the man she'd let her guard down over got her hopes right back up again. She had it bad for the guy, which meant one thing—she needed to get over it!

When she'd felt she'd spent the obligatory

amount of time mingling with the new doctors, inviting them to visit Pathology, and also with several of her staff colleagues, she decided to skip out, admittedly feeling disappointed. With no chance for witty conversation with her doctor of choice, that Southern charmer who appeared to be taken anyway, there was no point in sticking around another minute. Unfortunately, her path of exit brought her by Jackson and Yuri, who looked like they were edging their way out, too.

Yuri gazed at her, tension in her eyes. "Hi, Charlotte."

"Hi, Yuri." No hard feelings. Yuri was a nice woman. "See you Monday." She scurried on by but not before someone tapped her on the shoulder. A third time! That Antwan didn't know when to give up. She swung around, less-than-kind thoughts in her mind and probably flashing in her eyes, to see Jackson's laid-back smile.

"You going already?"

Switching gears fast, she skidded into sociable. "Oh, uh, yes. Got a big day tomorrow, with Dr. Gordon's surgery and all. Well, you obviously know that."

"Yeah, I'll be leaving shortly, too."

Hmm, he'd said "I'll," not "we'll." Stop it. Don't continue to be a fool. "Well, good-bye, then. I'll be ready with the cryostat bright and early. I promise to get those frozen sections cut, stained and read in record time."

"I'm sure you will. Well, listen, I just wanted to make sure you knew how stunning you look today. I could hardly take my eyes off you."

Was he saying this right in front of Yuri? What was with men these days? But Yuri smiled up at him approvingly.

"Well, thank you." Her head was officially spinning with confusion. "I guess." She glanced at Yuri again, who continued to smile. "Good-bye now."

Jackson grinned and nodded and let her leave with a wad of conflicting thoughts clumping up her brain. What was going on?

Once she hit the street and got some fresh air, she inhaled deeply to clear her head, then gave herself a stern talking-to. *That's what I get for letting a man get under my skin. I should know better!*

* * *

On Monday morning Charlotte came into work early, hoping to see Dr. Gordon in the hospital before he'd been given his pre-op meds. Unfortunately, he already had, but he wasn't yet so out of it that he couldn't squeeze her hand and give her a smile and a thumbs-up as they rolled him from his hospital room toward surgery. His slightly intoxicated grin nearly broke her heart.

The vision of him stripped down to a bland hospital gown, with a little blue "shower cap" covering over his abundant white hair, lying on the narrow gurney as the transportation clerk pushed him toward the elevator, made her eyes blur and her chest squeeze. It also brought back sad memories of seeing her mother in the same position years ago, and reinforced why she'd chosen the safety of the isolated pathology department to the hospital wards after medical school.

To distract herself, she stopped at the cafeteria and bought a large coffee, then headed to the basement to her department, where she'd double-check the cryostat before Dr. Gordon's first specimen arrived.

Jackson planned to send down from surgery a sentinel node for her initial study, and depending on her findings, they would proceed from there.

By eight-fifteen the OR runner appeared in her lab with the first node from Dr. Gordon. The specimen came with exact directions as to where it had been resected and she made a note of that with a grease pencil on the textured side of the first of several waiting glass slides. She carefully put the specimen in a gel-like medium and placed it in a mold for quick freezing in the cryostat. She helped the process along with special fast-freeze spray, then within less than half a minute mounted the fully frozen specimen on the chuck and set up the microtome to her exact specifications.

After dusting the initial cut away from the blade with a painter's brush, she made the next cut and got the full surface of the node on the microtome then pressed her labeled glass slide to pick it up. She used H&E stain for immediate results since the hematoxylin and eosin stains worked best for her purposes, then placed a coverslip.

Whisking the now stained slide to the lab microscope, she began her study, and soon her hope for a benign node was dashed. Within five minutes of receiving the first specimen, she had to report the bad news over the intercom that connected surgery to her little corner of the world. The protocol was not to get into histologic details with frozen sections, instead sticking to a "just the facts, ma'am" approach.

"Dr. Hilstead, this is Dr. Johnson reporting that the first lymph node is positive for metastatic cancer." The words tangled in her throat, and she had to force them out, refusing to let her voice waver in the process.

"I see," Jackson replied. "I'll proceed to the next lymph node. Stand by."

"I'll be here."

Jackson continued with abdominal lymph node dissection, and she dutifully and quickly made her cryosurgical cuts and examined each and every specimen under the microscope, tension mounting with each specimen. The head of histology poked her head in the door, wearing a sad expression. Word soon spread in the small laboratory section about Dr. Gordon. Charlotte worked on in silence. After three positive-for-cancer lymph nodes, her voice broke as she reported, "This one is also positive."

A lab tech standing silently behind her in the tiny cryostat room moaned and left, grabbing a tissue on the way out. Dr. Gordon was well liked by his staff because he treated everyone decently, and in Charlotte's case, taking her under his wing and mentoring her when she'd been a green-behind-the-ears pathologist. She owed so much to him, yet all she could do today was be the bearer of bad news on his behalf.

There was no hiding the fact her findings were tearing her up, and her favorite surgeon must have felt compelled to console her. "We're almost done here, Charlotte. Just a few more, I promise."

"Of course." She recovered her composure, knowing the entire surgical team could hear her over the intercom. "I'll be here, Doctor."

And so it went until they found a benign node after six specimens.

Early afternoon, stowed away in the comfort of her dark office, studying yesterday afternoon's surgical slides, Charlotte sipped chamomile tea. With her heart loaded down with emotions, feeling like a brick around her neck, it would be a long day that she'd just have to force herself through. She'd had plenty of experience willing herself through days at a time, beginning as a teenager and more recently two years ago after her surgery had been done and she'd had to deal with the reality of her decision. She'd stripped herself of part of her female identity and hadn't yet figured out how to move forward. Derek's reaction the first time they'd made love after surgery, his expression when he'd seen her, would forever be tattooed in her mind.

A light double tap on her closed door drew her out of the doldrums she'd been intent on wallowing in. "If it isn't important, I'd rather be left alone." She went the honest route, hoping the staff would understand, especially since they all seemed to already know about Dr. Gordon's diagnosis.

The door opened, and Jackson, ignoring her request to be left alone, stepped inside. He was still in OR scrubs, his wavy hair mostly covered with the OR cap as he closed the door behind him. "I thought you could use a friend right about now."

Not giving Charlotte a chance to respond, he walked to her desk, took one of her hands and, finding little resistance from her, pulled her to standing like a reluctant dance partner, then into his arms. He hugged her tightly and sincerely and the warmth washed over her like a comforting cloud, all soft and squishy, with every surface of her skin reacting to his embrace in goose bumps. Yes, she did need this, and Jackson had no idea how much it meant to her.

They stood together like that for several moments, her breathing in his scent and finding it surprisingly not sterile-smelling at all, even though he'd just come from surgery. She leaned into his solid body, enjoying it, knowing this was a man she could literally lean on. One of his hands wandered to her hair, as if unable to resist the opportunity to feel it. She liked that he was so obvious about it, and smiled against his shoulder.

Before standing in the dim light and holding each other became awkward, Jackson spoke. "Chemotherapy can work wonders these days.

I've already got Marv Cohen working on Jim's case, and I feel that already shifts the prognosis into a more positive direction."

Who was he kidding, trying to cheer her up? He was talking to a pathologist. She was a doctor from the end-of-the-road department where patients wound up after all the great medical plans hadn't panned out. The thing that hurt was that she knew Dr. Gordon himself had taught her to think that way. "We have to be realistic, Charlotte," he'd say. How would he feel when he woke up and got the news?

With all her dreary thoughts, she appreciated Jackson's desire to make her feel better. But this fight wasn't about her, it was Jim Gordon's to fight, and she promised she'd do everything in her power to help him. "I'll read the slides first thing in the morning, and report directly to Marv, after you, of course, so he can come up with a magic potion and stop this mess." *No matter what,* her mother had insisted to the very end, *don't lose hope.* Becoming a pathologist had made her cynical.

"I'm sure you will." His hands slid to either

side of her face, fingers gently cupping her ears. Then he studied her eyes. She'd never been this close to him before, and loved looking up into his angled features and, in her opinion, handsome face, into those often world-weary eyes. Distracted by the thickness of his eyelashes, she didn't see what was about to happen until his mouth lightly kissed hers. Surprising herself, she let him, relaxed and enjoyed the feel of his lips pressing on hers. This kind of comfort she could get used to really fast.

But wait. This couldn't happen! It meant things, like getting close to another human being again. A man. Which could lead to, well, sex. Which wouldn't happen because once Jackson found out about her surgery and the fact she'd stripped herself of many a man's favorite playground, the breasts, he'd be like Derek. Not able to accept her as she was—still a woman, but scarred and different.

The pain from Derek's walking away had sliced too deep.

She ended the kiss, not abruptly, just not allowing it to go any further. She prepared a quick cover, with a single thought planted in her head since yesterday. "Didn't I see you with Yuri yesterday?" By his confused expression, it seemed like she had the perfect antidote to stop this kiss cold.

"You did. I was doing her a favor."

Charlotte was very aware that even though they were no longer kissing, he hadn't let her out of his arms. "A favor?" Did he really expect her to believe that line?

"She's got a thing for Stan Arnold."

"The head of the medical lab?" Trying to picture petite Yuri with tall, gangly Stan made Charlotte smile.

"He would be the one. Apparently she's had a thing for him for years, and recently found out his wife had dumped him. So she cooked up this plan to make him jealous."

"I don't remember seeing Stan at the party yesterday."

"That's the joke. Yuri sets up this elaborate plan, me pretending to be her date, and the guy doesn't show up." He smiled and shook his head. "She's got it bad."

"I guess I shouldn't listen to everything Antwan tells me."

His eyes widened, as if amazed she'd listen to *anything* Antwan said, let alone everything. "Like what?"

"That you're a ladies' man, and you've dated a lot of women from St. Francis."

An odd look crossed his face. "Not at all true. I've had only a couple of dates since I've moved here, no one from the hospital, and once they got to know me, neither lady bothered to stick around." What was he telling her? Was there a Mr. Hyde to his charming Dr. Jekyll? Before she could delve into that loaded statement, Jackson spoke again. "And by the way, I noticed Dr. Dupree hanging around you a lot yesterday. If you hadn't already told me you don't have anything going on with him, I might have thought you were there together." He'd expertly changed the subject.

"Oh, no! I hope no one else thought that." She was well aware of still being in Jackson's arms, and was also dying to know if she'd made him feel jealous yesterday, even though she knew it was pointless, just a little ego bump.

"I don't really care what anyone else thinks, but *I'm* relieved." He kissed her again, this one far from a comfort kiss and sending shivers dripping down her spine. If she'd had any doubt about his interest before, he'd sure proved her wrong now. This kiss felt intimate, like they kissed like this every day, and she liked it. Kissing Jackson shut down her never-ending thoughts and questions, allowing her to stay in the moment and enjoy the soft yet persistent feel of his lips on hers. At first he kissed like a gentleman, but something she did—she'd got carried away and opened her mouth and pushed her tongue between his lips, to be exact—had fired him up. She reeled with the feel of him getting a little wild with the kisses because of something she'd set off. How long had it been since she'd done this to a man?

As his mouth worked down the side of her neck, finding many of her trigger points and setting loose chills, his hands began to wander over her shoulders and down her arms, soon skimming the sides of her chest down to her waist and back up.

As much as she was enjoying everything, he'd moved into "the zone" and it shocked her back to reality.

This can't happen. Not here. Not now. Not ever?

She pulled herself together and stepped back, letting him know they'd crossed a line for which she wasn't ready. She searched for and found her voice, barely able to whisper the words. "Though this is really nice, it probably isn't the best way to work out my concerns for Dr. Gordon."

"Seems like a pretty damn good replacement, though." Jackson, like the perfect gentleman that he usually had been until about five minutes ago, took a second to pull it together. "I'm pretty sure Jim will be out of Recovery by now. Want to go visit him with me?" It had been spoken as if nothing monumental had just happened between them, like he kissed women in their offices all the time.

"I'd love to." She'd also love to continue kissing him, but only in her dreams could she have what she really wanted from Jackson. Just like the reality of Dr. Gordon with metastatic cancer, some things weren't easily worked out.

With more questions about Jackson than she'd ever had before, and a boatload of mixed-up feelings, both mental and physical, for him, she still managed a daring last kiss. She'd call it a gratitude kiss. Granted, it followed a quick hug of thanks and was only a buss of the cheek, but at least it was something.

After graciously accepting her parting gift, and searching her stare for an instant, he headed for the door and she followed him toward the elevators for the post-op ward. Something significant had happened between them. Figuring out what it meant would be left for another time.

Before just now, never in her wildest imagination could she have seen that kiss coming.

Dr. Gordon's eyes were closed. The head of the hospital bed was elevated slightly, and the white over-starched sheets seemed to bleach what little color he had from his face. Oxygen through a nasal cannula helped his shallow breathing. The sight of her mentor looking so vulnerable made her stomach burn. She took his hand, the one with the IV, and his eyelids cracked open. He needed a few seconds to focus before he smiled.

"Hello, Jim. Glad to see you survived surgery," Jackson said, as if he'd had nothing to do with it.

"Yeah, some lunatic tried to kill me today." His gaze shifted to Charlotte rather than look at Dr. Hilstead any longer, and his tough facade softened as he did.

"How're you doing?" She could hardly hear herself.

"Besides feeling like I've been shot with BBs in my gut, okay, I guess."

"When was the last time you had pain medicine?"

"I lost track of time a while ago. I'm supposed to push this." He nodded toward the medicine dispenser attached to his IV pole, which allowed the patient to regulate pain control on the first day post-op. He pressed it. If enough time had passed since the last dose, he'd get more now, which of course would put him back to sleep.

"Can I give you some ice chips?"

"Sure." He let her feed the ice to him from a plastic spoon, and it struck her how over the past few years he'd spoon-fed her knowledge as her mentor. Helping now was the least she could do. She found a pillow on the bedside chair, fluffed it and exchanged it for the flattened one behind his head, just like she'd learned to do with her mother. He groaned with the movement but let her do it.

Their eyes met briefly. Appreciation, with flecks of hard-won wisdom, conveyed his thoughts. Jackson had probably already talked to him about the findings, and Dr. Gordon had assigned her to the frozen sections for the surgery. They all knew the outcome. There was no point in bringing it up.

She tried to keep sadness from coloring her gaze as they shared a sweetly poignant moment, almost like father and daughter. Emotion reached inside her and gripped until her throat tightened and she feared she'd start to cry. She inhaled as reinforcement. "You probably feel like sleeping."

He let her use the excuse, squeezed her hand one last time and let her go. "Thanks for coming by."

"I'll be back later, okay?"

He nodded, snuggled back on the pillow and shut his eyes again.

Jackson guided Charlotte at the small of her back from the bedside out the door to the nurses' station. "He knew before going in what the likelihood was of his having mets."

She hated this part of her job, verifying the worst outcome. Seeing her mentor's tired face just now, looking nothing like the strong head of the department she'd always looked up to, had knocked some of the air from her. She gulped and the swelling emotions she'd tried to ward off with little bedside tasks took hold. Her eyes burned, and her chest clutched at her lungs. Memories from nearly twenty years ago threw her to the curb, and she broke down.

Jackson swept her under his arm and walked her to a quiet side of the ward, back near the linen cart. "Let's go get a cup of coffee, okay?"

Trying her best to get hold of her runaway feelings, she nodded and swiped at her eyes. He handed her some nearby tissues, and she used them. Then, with his arm around her waist, he led her back to the elevator, which they had all to themselves.

"I didn't realize how close you are to Jim."

"He's been like a father figure to me. I lost my mother to breast cancer when I was fifteen, and my dad a few years after that. Dad just couldn't go on without her, I guess. I still miss them." Jackson's grasp tightened around her arm. "Dr. Gordon pretends he's an old grump, but I knew the first time I met him that he was a teddy bear. I guess I let him step into that vacant parental role. I don't know what I'll do—"

"Don't go down that path. We've got a lot of options at this point."

She nodded, further composing herself in preparation for their exit from the elevator. "My mother's missed diagnosis and subsequent illness was the reason I went into medicine and pathology."

"I wondered why a beautiful woman like you had chosen that department."

His honest remark helped lighten her burdens for the moment, and she smiled. He thought she was beautiful? "Do you think I'm ghoulish?"

It was his turn to grin, which definitely reached

his eyes, and he laughed a little, too. "I can safely say you and that word have never come to mind at the same time."

"Whew." She mock-wiped her brow. "Wouldn't want to make the wrong impression." *Because I really like you.*

They entered the cafeteria and, taking the lead, he grabbed a couple of mugs and filled them with coffee, after verifying with caffeine or not for her. Then he picked up a couple of cookies on a plate, and after he'd signed off on the charge, they went to the doctors' seating in a smaller and quieter room than the regular cafeteria. Leading the way, he chose a table and removed the items from the tray then waited for her to sit before he did. Yeah, a take-charge gentleman all the way.

"You feel like talking more about what tore you up back there?" He got right to the point.

She inhaled, poured some cream into her coffee and thought about whether or not she wanted to revisit those old sad feelings about her parents any more, and decided not to. "I'm good. Just worried about Dr. Gordon."

He reached across the table and squeezed her hand. "I understand."

She hoped her gratitude showed when their gazes met. From his reassuring nod she figured it did. She accepted a peanut-butter cookie and took a bite. "Mmm, this is really good."

He picked his up and dipped it in his black coffee before taking a man-sized bite. His brows lifted in agreement. "So," he said after he'd swallowed, "since we're going to change the subject, I have an observation. I'm thinking you might be dating someone?"

Her chin pulled in. "Why would you think that?" Hadn't they been making out in her office earlier?

"You put a quick stop to our..." He let her finish the sentence in her mind, rather than spell it out.

She lifted her gaze and nailed his, which was, not surprisingly, looking expectant. He was definitely interested in her, which caused thoughts to flood her mind. She'd gone through a long, tough day already, and it wasn't even two o'clock. She'd once again seen firsthand how things people took for granted, like their health, could change at any given moment. It made her think how much more out of life she longed for. Shouldn't she grab some of what it had to offer, especially when it, or rather, he, was sitting right across from her, dunking his cookie like it was the best thing on earth? Instead of day in and day out spending most of her time with the biggest relationship in her life, her microscope?

But would Jackson want her as she was? Admittedly, she'd always been proud of her figure, never flaunting herself too much but not afraid to show some cleavage if the occasion and the dress called for it. Now every day when she showered she saw her flat chest, the scars. There wasn't anything sexy about that. Yet she was a woman, lived, breathed and felt like a woman, but one who strapped on her chest the symbols of the fairer sex every day before she came to work. Pretending she was still who she'd used to be.

The decision had seemed so clear when she'd made it. Get rid of the tissue, the ticking time bomb on her chest. Never put herself in a position to hear the words that had devastated her mother's life. *You have breast cancer.*

Because of lab tests and markers, she'd thought like a scientist, but now she had to deal with the feelings of a woman who was no longer comfortable in her body.

Then there was tall, masculine and sexy-as-hell Jackson sitting directly across from her, smiling like he had a secret.

She bet his secret was nowhere as big as hers. "You took me by surprise earlier."

"I took myself by surprise."

She liked knowing that the kiss had been totally spontaneous. "So, since you asked, I'm not seeing anyone. Today's just been hard. That's why I—"

"I understand." His beeper went off. He checked it. "Let me know when you're leaving later and after we pop in on Jim again I'll walk you to your car."

It wasn't a question. She liked that about him, too. "Okay."

Except later, when Jackson walked her to her car, after visiting the hospital and finding Dr.

Gordon deeply asleep and looking like he floated on air, Jackson reverted to perfect-gentleman mode. No arm around her shoulder or hand-holding as they walked. Whatever magic they'd conjured earlier had worn off. He simply smiled and wished her good night, told her to get some rest, more fatherly than future boyfriend material, and disappointingly kept a buffer zone between them as she got into her car.

As she drove off, checking her rearview mirror and seeing him watch her leave, his suit jacket on a fingertip and hanging over his shoulder, looking really sexy, she wondered if he'd had time to come to his senses, too. Something—was it her?—held him back. Then, since she knew her secret backward and forward, and how it kept her from grabbing at the good stuff in life, she further wondered what his secret was.

CHAPTER THREE

JACKSON TOSSED HIS keys onto the entry table in his Westlake condo, thinking a beer would taste great about now, but knowing he'd given up using booze as an escape. It had cost what had been left of his marriage to get the point across.

A long and destructive battle with PTSD had led to him falling apart and quitting his position as lead surgeon at Savannah General Hospital just before they'd planned to fire him three years ago. The ongoing post-traumatic stress disorder had turned him into a stranger and strained his relationship with his teenage sons, frightening them away. It had also ensured his wife of twenty years had finally filed for divorce.

He'd lost his right lower leg in an IED accident in Afghanistan. It had been his second tour as an army reservist. He'd volunteered for it, and for that his wife had been unable to forgive him.

She'd deemed it his fault that the improvised explosive device had caused him to lose his leg. He'd returned home physically and emotionally wounded, and, piled onto their already strained marriage from years of him choosing his high-maintenance education and career over nurturing their life together, she couldn't take it.

His fault.

Their marriage had been unraveling little by little for years anyway. High-school sweethearts, she'd then followed him on to college. His grandfather used to tease him that she was majoring in marriage. Then they'd accidentally got pregnant the summer before he'd entered medical school. With their respective families being good friends, there was no way he could have let her go through the pregnancy alone. So he'd done the honorable thing and they'd got married right before he'd entered medical school.

It hadn't been long before they'd realized they may have made a mistake, but his studies had kept him too busy to address it, and the new baby, Andrew, had taken all of her time, and, well, they'd learned how to coexist as a small family of three. In his third year of medical school she'd got pregnant again. This time he'd got angry with her for letting it happen when he'd found out she'd stopped taking birth control pills. Evaline had said she wanted kids because he was never around. And so it had gone on.

Then at the age of twenty-seven and in the second year of his surgical residency, he'd signed up for the army reserves. One weekend a month he'd trained in an army field medical unit, setting up mobile triage, learning to care for mass casualties. When he'd finished his surgical residency and had been asked to stay on at Savannah General, his wife had thought maybe things would get better. But he'd started signing on with his reserve unit for two-week humanitarian missions for victims of natural disasters at home in the States. Soon he'd branched out to other countries, and when he'd been deployed to Iraq, Evaline had threatened to leave him.

He'd made it home six weeks later in one piece, his eyes opened to the need of fellow US soldiers deployed in the Middle East, and also finally accepting the trouble his marriage was in.

They seeked out marriage counseling and he'd focused on working his way up the career ladder at Savannah General, and things had seemed to get better between them. He'd stayed on in the army reserves doing his one weekend a month, catching hell from Evaline if it fell on either of his sons' sports team events, but he hadn't been able to pick and choose his times of service. They'd limped on, keeping a united front for their boys and their families, while the fabric of their love had worn thinner and thinner.

Then, after a brutal series of attacks on US military personnel, they'd needed army reserve doctors and he'd volunteered to be deployed to Afghanistan. He had been one week short of going home when the IED had changed everything.

His fault?

He'd come home, had hit rock bottom after that, then eventually had got help from the veterans hospital, and had spent the next year accepting he'd never be the man he'd once been and cleaning up his act. He'd been honorably discharged from the army, too. But the damage to Evaline and his sons and his reputation as a surgeon had already been done. She'd filed for divorce.

As time had passed his PTSD had settled down and he'd felt confident enough to go back to work. That was when he'd figured there wasn't anything for him back home in Georgia anymore. His wife had divorced him. His oldest son had wanted nothing to do with him. So since his youngest son would be attending Pepperdine University in Malibu, California, he'd sought employment in the area, hoping to at least mend that relationship. St. Francis of the Valley Hospital had been willing to give him a chance as a staff surgeon. With less responsibility, not being the head of a department but just a staff guy for a change, not having to deal with his ex-wife and her ongoing complaints anymore and enjoying the eternal spring weather of Southern California, his stress level had reached a new low.

Until today, when he'd had to tell his friend Jim Gordon some pretty rotten news—that he had metastatic cancer—and they both knew there'd be one hell of a battle ahead. Then, in a moment of weakness, seeing the distress Charlotte

Johnson had been in, he'd let his gut take over and he'd moved in to comfort her. But it hadn't worked out that way, because he'd played with fire. He knew he'd thought about her far, far differently than any other colleague. That he'd been drawn into her dark and alluring beauty while sitting across from her, looking at patient slides, for the last year. Come to think of it, could he have been any slower? How long had he had a thing for her anyway? At least three-quarters of the last year, that was how long.

Could he blame himself for kissing her when she'd fit into his arms so perfectly, and she'd shown no signs of resisting him? Still, it had been completely improper and couldn't happen again because he wasn't ready to have one more woman reject him because his lower leg had been replaced with a high-tech prosthetic. Maybe it wasn't sexy, but it sure worked great, and he'd been running five miles a day to prove it for the last two years. In fact, he'd never been in better condition.

Ah, but Charlotte, she stirred forgotten feelings, that special lure of a woman that made him want to feel alive again. Something about her mix of confidence on the job and total insecurity in a social setting made him hope what they had in common might be enough to base a new relationship on. When he'd kissed her, because of her response, he'd got his hopes up that maybe she felt the same way. But she'd stopped the kiss and an invisible barrier had seemed to surround her after that. He'd pretended everything had been fine when he'd walked her to her car—he hadn't noticed her need to be left alone—but the message had got through to him. Loud and clear.

He wandered into his galley kitchen and searched the refrigerator, hoping there might be something halfway interesting in the way of leftovers. He grabbed a bottle of sparkling water and guzzled some of it, enjoying the fizzy burn in his throat. Today he'd kissed the woman who held his interest more than any other since his high-school sweetheart. That was the good news. The bad news was he knew he couldn't do anything further about it. Her invisible force field wouldn't let him through, and if that wasn't enough, his boatload of baggage held him back.

Out of curiosity, though, he did have one little—okay, monumental—test for Charlotte, one
that would really determine her mettle before he
totally gave up.

Saturday was the annual charity fund-raiser five-
and ten-kilometer run for St. Francis of the Valley
trauma unit. Charlotte had signed up a while back
and had forgotten to train for it, but she showed
up anyway in support of the event. What they'd
neglected to tell her was that this year they'd
added zombies. Someone had got the bright idea
to raise more money by getting employees to pay
professional makeup artists, who'd donated their
time for the event, to be made up as the undead.
The sole purpose, besides getting their pictures
taken, was to chase down the runners and tag
them with washable paint, and hopefully improve
some personal best times for some participants
in the process.

Being a good sport, Charlotte ran with the
five-kilometer crowd, squealing and screaming
whenever zombies crawled out of bushes or from
behind nearby trees, heading straight for her. She

checked her sports watch. Out of fright she had cut her running time—well, the last time she'd run, which had been a month ago—by a couple of minutes at the halfway point. Impressive. Go zombies!

Running always made her think, and today was no different. Since Monday, with Dr. Gordon's surgery and the amazing kiss from Jackson, the man had been missing in action. He hadn't even shown up for their usual Friday afternoon slide show. Had the fact that she'd stopped him from kissing her the way he'd wanted been the reason? Or was her hunch right about him having his own reasons for keeping distance between them? She didn't have a clue, but one thing was certain—she missed him even though she felt safer when he wasn't around. Talk about being mixed up.

Oh, man, here came another small cluster of zombies, heading right for her and the group of three runners in front of her. The rules said that if a zombie left a red mark on you, you had to subtract thirty seconds from your final time. Even though she knew they weren't real, they still freaked her out. She shot into sprint mode and caught those runners up ahead, nestling herself in the middle of them as protection. She had no pride when it came to fear. They all screamed and swerved together as the slow-moving zombies up ahead got closer. They fanned out to avoid their zombie touch, especially if they carried red spray paint. She darted around another zombie, leaving the group of nurses behind and winding up running solo again, checking every bush and tree ahead for any surprises.

Soon things calmed down, so she slowed her pace and relaxed, enjoying the early morning sunshine and mild temperature. If she kept up like this she'd actually have a shot at finishing the run.

Already having finished his ten-kilometer race and finishing in the top twenty, Jackson had doubled back, deciding to run the five-kilometer route, too. He wasn't kidding himself. He knew that doing the shorter run as well had everything to do with searching for Charlotte, because he'd heard through Dr. Gordon she'd signed up to run.

Up in the distance he saw a woman with

long legs and rounded hips, wearing tight running gear, with a high ponytail swishing back and forth with each stride. Her lovely light olive-colored legs and arms helped make the call that, yes, it was undeniably Charlotte. She wasn't what he'd call a sporty type, but was fit for sure, though with full-figure curves, and in his mind she looked fantastic. Man, he'd missed her this week and really liked spying on her now.

He picked up his pace, realizing there was no hiding his big secret since he was wearing jogging shorts. He'd noticed the looks all morning from hospital employees as he'd sprinted by with his carbon graphite transtibial prosthetic, including a flex foot that looked suspiciously like the tip of a snow ski. Their interest in his running blade didn't bother him, he'd had to get used to it over the past couple of years, but that little yet monumental test he was about to give Charlotte—finally finding out what she'd think of his prosthetic and below-the-knee amputation—made his stomach tighten.

He hoped she wouldn't be like the only two women he'd dated since moving out West, neither of whom had been able to get past his missing leg. He'd once played the pity-me game and had lost his marriage and family, and since then had promised himself to never let it affect him again. So why was he so nervous now, jogging up behind Charlotte?

Well, here goes nothing. He lunged forward and reached out then grabbed her shoulder.

A hand grabbed Charlotte's shoulder. She screamed and nearly jumped out of her highly padded sports bra. Being so close to the finish line, would she be disqualified by a fake zombie bite?

With her heart nearly exploding in her chest, she turned to see how ugly the zombie who'd taken her out was. Instead she found a face that managed to take what was left of her breath away. It was Jackson's, and she wanted to throttle him!

"You nearly gave me a heart attack," she squeaked, soon forgiving him when she noticed those broad shoulders and the fit physique beneath the tight T-shirt, and how handsome he looked in the early morning sunshine, his hair damp and curling around his face from his workout. She smiled.

"Sorry, couldn't resist it." He slowed down his pace to stay with her.

"Well, I'm amazed I've made it this far without being attacked."

"I'll protect you."

Oh, how those amazingly masculine words put new spring in her step. She couldn't resist and took a quick glance at his shorts and those strong athletic legs. And, holy cow, the man had a prosthetic limb! And he ran like an Olympic athlete, with smooth, even strides and barely any effort at all, not out of breath in the least. He looked like a wounded warrior running on that shiny high-tech blade.

Her mind worked at laser speed. He usually came to her office wearing scrubs or street clothes. Once or twice she'd noticed his masculine arms, muscles that'd come from weights at the gym, but she'd never had the opportunity to see his amazing abdomen and those runner's muscled legs. Had she mentioned, holy cow, that he had a below-the-knee amputation on the right?

That explained his slightly unusual gait.

So her crush for the better part of a year had been on a man who had more in common with her than she could have ever dreamed! They were both missing something. The next question was, why had he grabbed her just now, obviously slowing down his pace to run with her?

It had to be because he liked her, too. Hadn't he proved it Monday afternoon when they'd hugged and kissed? The fact that he'd stayed far away from her and her department ever since, so very unlike him, had made her think differently and had proved he had reservations about starting a relationship. Welcome to the club, buddy. At least now she understood why and it didn't hurt so much that he'd been avoiding her. But it scared her, and not in a zombie-chasing way but much deeper. Because it was as plain as the sun right there in the sky making her squint. This. Was. A. Test.

She took another glance at his leg, more blatant this time, keeping her expression blasé, and making sure he noticed. Then she acted like there was absolutely nothing unusual about him.

He gave her a relaxed smile. She noted relief in

his gaze, letting on how much he appreciated her casual acceptance of his amputation. Yeah, her mind was spinning out of control in record time with thoughts and deductions, but she couldn't help it. This was such a surprise. And it leveled the playing field, which sent a shiver across her skin, warm and damp from running almost five kilometers.

"So now you know," he said matter-of-factly, sounding like it was a challenge.

Think fast for the perfect answer, because if there was ever a time for the right words, it was now. She tried not to remember how cutting Derek's words had been to her the first time he'd seen her chest. *That's pretty extreme, Charl, and to think it wasn't even necessary.* Who was she kidding? It wasn't just what he'd said but the shocked, nearly horrified and unaccepting expression that had accompanied it. Pain radiated through her chest as all these thoughts and memories flashed past in less than a second. Think fast! *He's waiting for a response to his comment.* "That you're not perfect? I think I already knew that, Doctor, the day you said you didn't like my all-time-favorite chocolate bars."

He laughed, and she felt good about dismantling the bomb he'd expected to leave her with.

Then, like the fact he was missing part of a leg meant nothing, they forgot about it and ran on, Jackson prodding her along and scooping her away from another zombie attack as they closed in on the last half-kilometer mark. For someone who hadn't trained, she'd make sure to finish this race if it killed her, rather than let her new running partner down.

"I take it you run a lot," she said, having to gasp the words since she was so out of breath.

"It's the best stress reliever I know."

"Hey, Dr. Hilstead, isn't this your second time around?" one of the OR techs called from the crowd on the sidelines as they approached the finish line.

"I'm helping my friend be safe from the zombies," he shouted back.

"Wait, so you've already finished this race?"

"I ran the ten kilometers." He looked straight ahead, rather than rub it in with a self-satisfied look.

Yeah, I run five in my sleep. She mocked how

she figured what his smug thoughts were about now, though using the last of her quickly disappearing breath. Now she'd have to finish this race even if she had to crawl over the line, just to save face.

He laughed again, and she was happy a guy who'd taken a big chance and shown the entire hospital his secret was in such a good mood. She hoped she'd had something to do with it, too, because she wanted to think the biggest risk he'd taken had been with her reaction. That would make her special, and she'd passed with flying colors. She hoped so anyway. Was she special?

"Got any steam left?" he asked. "Let's finish strong."

She understood the "let's" meant "her" and he wanted her to kick it up for the next several meters. Typical guy. Show him a finish line and he'd have to make a run for it.

She nodded, lying, and pushed into a sprint, well, her version of a sprint anyway—no hint of form, arms nearly flailing and her feet kicking up in a girlie run way behind her. But in her world she finished strong, simply because she finished!

He grinned and grabbed her shoulder again, this time not scaring the life out of her but guiding her to the SAG station for water and a banana. Her knees were wobbly, she gulped for air, and her pulse tore through her chest, but other than that she felt great.

"Good job, Dr. Johnson!" several of the hospital volunteers said in unison.

She wasn't able to speak just yet, so she smiled and sipped some water to prove she was still alive. Jackson stood there grinning at her, his chest hardly moving, only a sheen of exertion on his skin. She, on the other hand, was sweating big fat drops, her sports bra with the "natural-looking" silicone padding nearly sliding out of place. He nabbed a towel from the volunteers' table and put it around her neck.

"Thanks." She could finally talk.

"You did great."

"You made me."

"Then I'm glad I found you."

Oh, the things she could imagine with that statement. *I'm glad I found you.* Wait, he'd been looking for her? Further proof he might be interested, and now that she'd passed the test, why not go for it? She'd finished the run, was now high on endorphins, or was it light-headedness from low blood oxygen? Who cared? She felt good right now, and she could talk again, so she decided to go for it. "Hey, you want to have dinner with me later?"

After all they'd been through together for the last few minutes—his surprise test, her passing it, his forcing her to excel at a sport she could honestly live without, her probably setting a new "slowest five-kilometer" world record, him acting proud of her anyway, and probably for many reasons—he hesitated.

Every part of his facial expression put on the brakes, and it took her aback. So she thought fast and covered. "I've got an autopsy to do later this afternoon, and I thought if you weren't doing anything around five, you might join me in the cafeteria for a quick and easy dinner? Nothing special or anything. No big deal." Had that sounded professional enough? It was nothing like a *date* date, just dinner with a running buddy who'd shown her his BKA for the first time today.

Jackson's mind wandered in a half-dozen different directions. Why was a great and attractive girl like Charlotte spending Saturday afternoons doing autopsies and offering last-minute dinner invitations? Hell, yeah, he wanted to spend time with her, but tonight was a rescheduling of his usual Friday night dinner and a movie with his son. He couldn't back out from that, they still had too much to work through, and things continued to be strained. But they were making progress. His son attending Pepperdine had been his main motive for moving to California in the first place. What was left of his family had to come first.

Reality clicked in. Tonight wasn't the night. His fascination with the lovely pathologist, who now knew about his leg, would have to wait.

"Can I take a rain check on that invitation?"

James, the near-to-retirement morgue attendant, was ready and waiting after Charlotte had showered and changed into scrubs. By the time she'd donned the gown, shoe covers, face mask and clear plastic face shield, plus two pairs of gloves, he'd already weighed the body and placed it on the stainless-steel gurney-style table, complete with irrigation sink and drainage trough. A large surgical table was nearby with the tools of her trade—bone saw, rib cutter, hammer with hook, scalpel, toothed forceps, scissors, Stryker saw and more.

A family had requested an autopsy on their loved one, a twenty-five-year-old man, who'd arrived in the hospital three days earlier with signs of a bacterial infection. The hospital had agreed to the postmortem examination to identify any previously undiagnosed condition that may have contributed to his death, and to pin down what bacterium had suddenly run rampant throughout his system.

As a clinical pathologist, not to be confused with forensics like people saw on TV dramas just about every night of the week, her job was to see for herself what may or may not have caused his death. Knowing that up to a quarter of performed autopsies revealed a major surprise other than the notated cause of death, over the next two to four hours she'd systematically examine the outside and inside of this young man's body to get to the best and most logical diagnosis.

James, her diener, stood by ready to assist with each aspect of the autopsy. Turning on her Dictaphone, Charlotte described what she saw externally. Then she used a scalpel to make a Y-shaped incision. Before her afternoon was done she'd weigh and measure every major organ, take systematic biopsies and place them in preservation solution. She'd also collect blood and fluid for laboratory specimens, snap pictures and preserve the brain in fixative for future dissection. She wondered what the zombies would think of her now.

James labeled as they went along and would, after the autopsy, submit all specimens to the histology lab for Monday, when they resumed their work week. Once the autopsy was complete, James would wash the body and make it ready for the funeral home.

Though the family might want and expect immediate results, like they'd come to expect on those infamous TV dramas, it might be an entire month before she'd have the final report completed. Autopsies needed and deserved the extra time to make the right diagnoses.

Her beeper went off. Ah, damn, it was Dr. Dupree. Since he'd called on her official hospital beeper, she answered.

"I need a favor," he said, before she could even say hello.

She'd grown to expect the worst whenever Antwan said he needed anything. "Yes?"

"They told me you're on call, and I just got an okay from a family for an autopsy. Can you do it for me tonight?"

"Tonight? Why the rush?"

"The family gave me twenty-four hours until they send their daughter to the mortuary. I need this favor, please."

She wasn't used to hearing sincerity in his voice. "When did the patient die?"

"Just now. I operated on her two weeks ago. Removed her appendix. Everything went great. Two days ago she was readmitted for loss of consciousness at home. Medicine was doing a workup on her. She seemed to be fine. Then a nurse found her unresponsive in the hospital bed. She was already dead."

"Okay. Send her to the morgue. I'll tell James about the add-on."

"Thank you. I owe you a special dinner out."

"No, you don't. This is my job." Why was it that every time she spoke to Dr. Dupree her hackles rose? Because he was such a player, hitting on every woman in a skirt or hospital scrubs. But just now he'd shown a new side, genuine caring for a young patient who'd died of mysterious causes that may or may not have had something to do with the recent surgery. He was either being extra thorough or covering his backside... CYA, as the saying went.

For the sake of the family and the concerned doctor, Charlotte would do her usual thorough examination, and if she got lucky tonight, she might solve an unfortunate mystery.

Four hours later, having completed the long and complicated second autopsy, with strong suspicions that the young female patient had most likely died from an undetected brain aneurysm, she opted to shower in the doctors' lounge. It was nearly ten by the time she was dressed and ready to go home, but she decided to make a quick stop at her office first to call Security.

The elevator dinged as she unlocked the door to the pathology department, which was a few doors down from the morgue. She glanced over her shoulder in case it was Security, in which case it would save her a call, but out came Jackson. Though tired from a long day, her mood immediately lifted.

"Hi," he said, looking as surprised as she was. "I took a chance and got lucky."

"Hi, yourself. What are you doing here?" She unlocked the door and opened it. He followed her inside.

"I realized I didn't have your personal cellphone number, and thought I'd see if you were still around so I could get it."

He'd come back to the hospital at...she glanced at her watch...ten-fifteen p.m., hoping to run into her? Sure, she was happy the man was pursuing her, but it also made her wonder about his dinner date. She gave him her number and watched as he entered it into his cell phone. Then he insisted she take his. A good sign.

"How'd the autopsy go?"

"I wound up doing two."

"No kidding. You must be beat."

"Yeah, it's been a long day, starting with getting chased by zombies and ending with, well, you know." Out of respect for the dead she always recalled the Latin phrase—*Hic locus est ubi mors gaudet succurrere vitae. This is the place where death rejoices to help those who live.* It was her way of reframing the tough job she did as a pathologist, especially when both of the autopsies she'd performed tonight had been on young people, which always seemed wrong.

His hand came to her shoulder and lightly massaged. "Yeah, I know. It must be hard."

"No harder than what you do in surgery." She turned and looked up at him. Though he stood behind her, she got the distinct impression he might like to kiss her again, and admittedly, with that warm hand caressing her tight shoulder muscle, the thought appealed.

But he didn't. "You've got a point. Why don't

I stick around while you do whatever you've got to do? Then I'll walk you to your car."

The rule at St. Francis Hospital was for every female employee—or any employee who preferred to be escorted, for that matter—to call Security after dark for the walk to the parking lot. Charlotte had used the service many times. In fact, it was the sole reason she'd come back to her office, to make the call and wait until a security guard arrived. Now she wouldn't have to.

"Thanks for saving me a call to Security. It usually takes twenty minutes for anyone to show up, so I was going to look at a few slides while I waited."

"I'll stick around if you still want to check those slides."

"To be honest, I'd really like to get home."

"Let's go, then."

As they walked, Charlotte couldn't let her question remain silent. "So how'd your evening go?"

"It was good. I had dinner with my youngest son, Evan—or Ev, as he prefers to be called these days."

Relieved that his mysterious dinner date had

been with his son, she smiled. "You get together often?"

"Yeah, usually on Friday nights, but he had other plans last night."

So that was who he rushed off to every Friday afternoon. Her spirits kept lifting with each tidbit of information Jackson dropped. "That's great." And she really meant it.

He grimaced. "Well, we've got a lot to work out. The divorce was hard on both my sons but particularly on Evan. I've got to rebuild his trust, and we're getting there little by little."

She admired how much Jackson's family meant to him. It put him in a good light—a man who loved his family. The more she learned about him the more she liked, and the fact he had a BKA had zero impact on his appeal. If only she could trust that her situation would be as easily dealt with by him as his was for her. Unfortunately, her experience with Derek had set her up to expect the worst.

Sooner than she expected, because they always found conversation easy, he delivered her to the car.

"So thanks, and good night, then," she said, and as she unlocked the door and prepared to slide behind the wheel, he pecked her on the cheek. It surprised her, but in a good way, though she'd kind of wished for more and sooner than now.

"So I'll call you later, okay?"

"Sure." She grinned, enjoying being pursued by a man she was definitely attracted to. Maybe that was why the second part of her thought slipped out. "I'd really like that."

From the look on his face, he really liked that, too. Good!

Once inside her car, as she placed the seat belt over her shoulder and across her chest, her elation ebbed a bit. What was she thinking, acting like she was just a regular woman living a regular life, hoping to have a regular relationship with a new guy? That was ancient history for her—love, marriage, a career and family—a dream she could never achieve now.

Mindlessly, her hand brushed over her silicone pads. She was anything but regular.

But forty-five minutes later, when Charlotte was home and in her pajamas, Jackson didn't waste any time before using his newly acquired phone number. He said he'd called just to make sure she'd got home okay and to bid her good night again. She went to bed wearing a smile and thinking of his handsome face. Maybe taking a risk on a man like Jackson made perfect sense. Who could possibly be better than a guy with a BKA to understand her sense of feeling incomplete?

CHAPTER FOUR

MONDAY MORNING, CHARLOTTE visited Dr. Gordon, who was still in the hospital. He was undergoing aggressive chemotherapy and the oncological team decided it would be best for him to be monitored round the clock for the first couple of doses.

She put on her optimistic face, hoping her mentor didn't see right through her, since she secretly worried the therapy might be too little too late. Surprisingly, Dr. Gordon seemed in good spirits, and though the chemo had to be tough on him, he didn't complain.

Already Charlotte could see his hair and white caterpillar fuzzy brows thinning, the shine in his always inquisitive hazel eyes dulled. Memories of her mother losing her beautiful light brown hair nearly broke her heart, and how toward the end a raging fever had changed her mother's eyes to a glassy stare. At moments like these, the harsh reminders, she was glad she'd had the radical surgery to ensure she'd never have to go through what her mother had. Deep down she also knew there was no guarantee against cancer.

Charlotte fluffed Dr. Gordon's pillow, assuring him his department hadn't yet gone to hell in a handbasket, to use one of his favorite phrases, thanks to a few other pathologists pitching in along with her to cover for him. She gently replaced the pillow behind his head.

"I would expect no less, Charlotte," he said gratefully. "I only mentor the best and brightest."

His confidence in her skills had always amazed her, and right now a warm sense of fondness expanded to the limits of her chest as she made sure his call light was within reach and the pitcher of ice water was nearby. "Thank you," she said, fighting back the tears that always threatened whenever she was around him these days.

"No." He inhaled, as if continuing to talk would soon be a burden. "Thank you." He gave a frail squeeze of her hand and she leaned forward and kissed his forehead.

"Don't tell anyone I did that."

He winked. "It'll be our secret."

She smiled and quickly left because her vision was blurring and she didn't want Dr. Gordon to see her cry. No sooner had she stepped outside his room than her cell phone vibrated. It was Jackson. She headed for the elevator and answered.

"Have dinner with me," he said the instant after she answered. "We'll call it our rain check. I've found a great place in Westlake and it's no fun to eat out by myself."

Well, it wasn't exactly the most romantic offer for a date, but she liked it that he'd thought of her. "Tonight?"

"Got plans?"

"I've got extra work to clear out, what with Dr. Gordon being off, and—"

"Tomorrow night, then. We'll take a rain check on our rain check."

It only took a second to make her decision. "That should work. Sure, I'd love to."

"Great! I'll need your address."

The guy clearly wasn't big on chitchat. Did she

want him coming to her town house in Thousand Oaks to pick her up? If he was any other first date, or someone like Antwan, she'd insist on meeting somewhere. On second thought, she'd never consent to meeting Dr. Dupree anywhere! But this was Jackson Hilstead the Third, her secret crush, the one guy in the hospital who might possibly understand her fragile body image, because he'd fought the same demons. "What time?" she asked, after giving him her street address.

"Seven."

"That'll work."

She hung up, grinning, her mind whirring. She had a little over twenty-four hours to clear her desk, clean up her house and find something sexy but not too revealing to wear. She hadn't been this excited about going out with a man in a long time.

Now, if she could just ignore that insecure whisper, *He won't accept you as you are*, starting up in her mind and concentrate on enjoying herself on their first date. Her first date in…she couldn't remember when.

* * *

Jackson finished his Tuesday afternoon surgery early and made hospital rounds on his patients, updating the doctor's orders on some and discharging a few others. Feeling a long-forgotten ball of excitement winding up inside over the thought of dinner with Charlotte, he grinned all the way to his car. He'd take a long run as soon as he got home to work off the edge. He hadn't looked forward to getting to know a woman like this in a long time.

He'd dated a couple of different women over the last year in California when he'd been feeling lonely and had needed a woman's company. His self-image had taken a serious hit when he'd lost part of his leg. But then, he hadn't expected to get a divorce at the time either. And when it had become obvious that his two dates hadn't been ready for an imperfect guy, he'd stopped looking around, because the rejections only a few months apart and the subsequent effect on his ego had turned out to be major. He'd been in the prime of his life and the thought of being alone from here on out had sometimes been too depressing to consider. So he'd pushed his feelings down and had gone about his days working hard and trying to put things right with his sons.

And he'd hated to admit it wasn't enough. Enter Charlotte.

He'd always taken solace in the safe haven of Dr. Charlotte Johnson's office. Reading slides with her had turned into his one indulgence with the opposite sex in the last year. He liked sitting close enough to notice whatever new perfume she chose to wear, and to catch the fire in her rich caramel-brown eyes whenever she found something interesting on one of his patients' slides to share with him. He liked it that she didn't lead with her sex, like so many other women around the hospital. They had it and they flaunted it, and it often made his basic urges get all fired up, which sometimes made it hard to concentrate.

Did a man ever grow out of that? He was forty-two, so apparently not.

But Charlotte was different. She had a fuller figure than many of the women at St. Francis Hospital, which he preferred to a woman being too thin, and though she dressed in a very feminine way, she was careful not to show too much skin. That made her interesting, and alluring in a far less blatant way than the others. Call it intriguing. But what appealed to him most of all was her no-nonsense personality. She clearly had her head on straight, and after the long, slow decline and eventual implosion of his marriage, when his wife had seemed to become his worst nightmare—granted, he'd turned into a nightmare of his former self, too—that was a welcome change. With a woman like Charlotte, maybe he could learn to trust again.

Was that asking too much?

Even the thought sent a shiver down his spine. Could he survive another rejection? Sure, she'd seen his leg and had acted as though she couldn't care less, and she'd accepted his dinner invitation, another good sign. But she was a nice woman who happened to be a pathologist and who'd probably seen it all in her job. Of course she wouldn't have let on if she'd felt disgust. He knew that much about her.

A memory of his wife finally telling him how

much he repulsed her, even when he'd already known it, made his stomach burn.

He needed to make sure this date wasn't taken out of context. Yes, he wanted to get to know Charlotte more, see where it might lead, but there wasn't anything he could offer beyond that. He wasn't ready for anything else. Small steps. His policy was always honesty, so tonight he planned to put his cards on the table and see what she thought.

Keep things safe. Keep her at a distance. Protect himself.

He had to, otherwise he couldn't go through with the date.

Jackson picked up Charlotte at seven on the dot, fighting a swarm of jitters in his gut. Hell, he hadn't felt this nervous about a date since his high-school prom—and he'd taken his ex-wife as his date to that! *Man up, Hilstead. It's just dinner out. With a lady you can't seem to get out of your thoughts.*

He forced his best smile, even though he'd only made it to the security call box.

Once she let him through, he strode the rest of the way to her town house, wondering if he'd made a mistake in asking her out. Maybe it was still too soon to get back in the game. Damn the nerves—how was he supposed to eat with his stomach all tied up?

Then Charlotte opened the door and blew him away. She'd worn her hair down, which always messed with his head. It waved and tumbled to her shoulders, framing her face and highlighting her warm and inviting eyes. Plus she'd dressed to kill in a cream crocheted lace dress with a modest neckline and cap sleeves. Her light olive-toned skin blended well with the choice. The only color in her outfit was from her rainbow-dyed strapped wedge sandals and bright red and orange dangly earrings. As it was early summer, she'd fit right in for the restaurant he'd chosen.

She smiled and let him in and he pretended he wasn't the least bit anxious about this date. He just hoped she didn't catch on.

Her earth-toned, stucco-covered townhome was built into the side of a hill along with dozens of others. The place had a nice view of the

Conejo Valley sprawl, and he was impressed with her taste in decor. No overstuffed and patterned couches or chairs, her taste was modern, clean and almost masculine. Several canvases covered in bright colors highlighted a few walls, and he recognized the style as similar to many he'd seen in the hospital foyer after it had been newly re-modeled. He vaguely remembered hearing that one of the employees had painted them, and these looked very similar in style. Seeing the paintings on Charlotte's walls, adding vibrancy to her otherwise beige palate, he wholeheartedly agreed with her choices.

But what he noticed most of all, and constantly since stepping into her house, was her, and how fantastic she looked.

She'd grabbed her purse and was ready to leave, so he quit staring at the view from her living room—because the alternative was to keep staring at her, which he really wanted to do, but he didn't want to creep her out—then followed her out the door. He'd better think up some conversation or he'd be a total dud tonight. What was his plan? Oh, yeah, lay his cards on the table.

Take control of the situation from the get-go. He could do it.

"Ever hear of a place called Boccaccio's?" he asked as they walked to his car in the building's lot.

"In Westlake? Yes. Wow, it's supposed to be really nice. Are you trying to impress me?"

"I should be asking the same question, seeing how great you look." She blushed and he not only liked how she looked, but the power her true response gave him. He could do this, have a date. "But don't get too impressed. Yes, the restaurant is right on a small lake and, yes, the view is great, but it's just a man-made lake in an otherwise landlocked city."

"Still sounds wonderful to me. I'll just pretend it's real. Can we sit outside?"

"I was planning on it."

She was tall and fit well next to his six feet two inches as they walked to his white sedan. So many things about her appealed to him, but he had to stand firm, let her know what he was and wasn't open to. Keep that arm's length between them, though after seeing her all decked out tonight, the thought was becoming less appealing. After they'd uncorked a bottle of wine and shared a meal together, maybe she'd understand why he needed to do things his way. He hoped so anyway.

Once they'd arrived at the restaurant, having talked about work and Dr. Gordon the entire drive over, his unease had settled down somewhat. As it was a Tuesday night they didn't have long to wait to be seated outside. It was twilight, a gorgeous summer evening, and the small lake was tinted with a peach hue as the sun said good-bye for the day. There really was something special about Californian sunsets. Charlotte was impressed, he could tell by the bright expression on her face, and how she craned her neck to take in the view from every angle, and he thought it was cute. The choice of word struck him as odd for a woman who was so much more than cute, but something in the way she crinkled her nose with delight over her surroundings put it in his head.

"I've heard good things about this place. Now I understand why."

"The food is supposed to be as good as this

view." So far his conversation had been stiff as
hell. He ordered a bottle of a good sauvignon
blanc with her approval, and they set about making their dinner choices. They ordered calamari,
light and crispy, for starters to share. Next he
ordered a salad and she lobster bisque. For the
main, she chose baby salmon piccata, and he
went for the Chilean sea bass. Then the waiter
left and the sommelier poured their wine.

He sat back and relaxed in the comfortable
woven wicker and wrought-iron chair, thought
about stretching out his legs but realized he'd
bump her with his prosthesis if he did, so he
stayed sitting straight up. He glanced across the
table at his date, who continued to enjoy the view
of the small lake and the early evening lights
around the shore.

Charlotte was his date. Wow, that was a new
concept. She was pretty and so damn appealing, enough to shake him up all over again. She
sipped her wine and he joined her. The sweet
smile she offered him afterward warmed his insides far more than the wine. She could be dangerous. He took another drink.

"I should let you know that I haven't wanted to impress a woman this much in a long time." His honesty surprised even him.

She canted her head and gave a self-deprecating simper.

"But I've got to be honest, okay?" Build that wall.

Her intelligent eyes went serious.

"I've already told you I'm divorced, but you should also know it was a really bad one. So the thing is I'm looking for companionship, but I can't promise anything beyond that." *Oh, right, buddy, lay it on* her—*don't dare admit* you're *a coward.*

She didn't seem surprised by his opening statement, though he'd half expected her to be, and honestly, it did seem more like the opening remarks in a court of law rather than dinner with a great woman. "This is just our first date, so I'm on the same page."

Who was he kidding, trying to pull this off? What had happened to honesty? "I'm probably coming off like an ass, but I respect you too much to not be open." He leaned on the table, looked her in the eyes. "I'm not sure I ever want to get into a serious relationship again, not after what I've been through. I don't see myself ever marrying again, and I definitely don't want to be a father again."

She took another drink of her wine. "Hold on a second. Let's not get ahead of ourselves."

He had to laugh. He was jumping way ahead of a first date. "Yeah, I get that, but I think it's better to put it out there right up front." Wouldn't someone like her want the whole package, a career and a family?

"So now there are pre-dating rules, sort of like pre-nups? I guess I've been out of the loop awhile."

He laughed again, this time at how absurd he must have sounded. What a jerk he was being. Would she want to spend another second with him? He should have left well enough alone and never asked her out. But their kiss and the feelings she'd brought back to life for him had made him pursue her. Yeah, he still wanted that. He had to be honest with himself first.

Luckily the waiter delivered their starter and

they spent the next minute or two distracted, sorting out sharing the appetizer. He took a bite and grinned over the taste of calamari done just right, surprised he could eat with the hard knot of nerves in his stomach. At least the food service was going well.

After she'd finished her part of the appetizer, she wiped her mouth and took another sip of wine. "I hear what you're saying, and that you're going out of your way to make sure I understand it. I get it. I know you've been there, done that, and you probably think I think my biological clock is telling me it's time to have babies." She swirled the half glass of wine round and round. "I'm thirty-four after all. So you figure you need to take the stars out of my eyes, not let me get any ideas. But I've also got reasons for not wanting kids. So don't worry about me getting any ideas about a long-term relationship. I'll be honest and say I like your company and I'd like to spend more time with you, but I don't plan to have children or, for that matter, get married either. Deal?"

Surprised she'd just released him from any future involvement, besides feeling relieved by her blunt answer, he wondered why a young and vibrant woman such as her would have ruled out marriage or having kids. Not with him necessarily, but with anyone. His laying his cards on the table had backfired, planting more questions in his mind than answers. "I wasn't suggesting we'd rush into anything."

"And I definitely don't want to rush into anything before I'm ready either."

If he had any question about what she'd been referring to before, he understood now. She'd like to date but not be intimate. At least, that was what he assumed her message had been. "I can understand that." Had he subconsciously been thinking about being intimate with her? Of course he had, but he'd already figured out he wasn't nearly ready for that. She'd probably read his mind and cut him a break. But, honestly, who in their right mind would want to get involved with him after all he'd just said?

Glancing at her in the evening light, with tiny decorative string lights in the background outlining her head like a sparkly crown, making her look even more beautiful, he wished he was ready to be with a woman again. Her.

"And just in case you're wondering, it has nothing to do with your leg." She interrupted his quickly shifting thoughts, and he was glad of it. She'd brought up his leg, or rather his missing leg, the elephant in the room. Good. "My hesitation comes from my side of things. For personal reasons. Though I do want to hear how you lost your leg, and anything else you ever feel like talking about." She reached across the table and touched his hand. "I really want us to be friends."

"Friends?"

"Let's see where that leads, okay? No pressure on either side."

He could live with that, if it meant he got to spend more time with Charlotte. "Fair enough."

Salad and soup arrived and Jackson poured another glass of wine for both of them. Since he figured they'd already ironed things out, he relaxed and enjoyed the company of a woman who turned out to be as witty and warm as she was great looking. But he'd already known that, and that was what scared the daylights out of him.

The words from an Adele song popped into Charlotte's head. She'd once played it over and over after Derek had broken her heart. *This man would never let her or any woman close enough to hurt him again.* Jackson was proving to be a true wounded warrior, right to the core. Keep her at a distance. Keep things safe. Take control right from the start. Very military or surgeon-like. And she thought she had a stick up *her* back. Whew. Jackson was hurting hard. She finished the last of her wine—he was driving after all.

But she still liked him, and could totally relate to what he'd suggested. Admittedly, at first when he'd started his spiel she'd thought, *Step away from the walking wounded. This guy is not for you.* But after savoring dinner and getting past the rule book, she'd enjoyed the evening out. He'd even opened up and told her how an IED had blown off his leg while killing two of his medical team and injuring a dozen others in the midst of performing surgery in Afghanistan. Maybe they could be good for each other. Why not give this a try? If he wanted safety and distance, in her current insecure state she was more than down with that.

When they arrived back home and he walked her to the security gate, he surprised her by stealing a kiss. She liked his surprises, and slipped right into the mood. He was a good kisser, and she liked putting her arms around his neck, leaning into him. Really kissing him. Close like this, could he tell her chest was different than real breasts?

Damn. She'd ruined the moment.

She dropped away from their kiss, seeing a hunger in his eyes that, to be honest, frightened her. What happened to safety and distance? His rules.

"Thanks for a great dinner and a lovely evening."

His waning smile was tinted with chagrin. "Thanks for putting up with me."

"I like you, Jackson. You get that, right?"

"I do, and despite the mess I made of things earlier, I'm really glad you do." He dropped his forehead to hers, the intimacy of the act seeming out of the boundaries of his dating playbook. "I like you, too." She didn't pull away, just kept her arms resting on his solid shoulders, gazing at his eyes up close. "You want to catch dinner together at the hospital tomorrow before you go home?"

An odd offer, but...

"Or we could go out for a quick meal."

Had he read her mind?

"I've got surgeries up the wazoo on Thursday, need to buckle down and mentally go over the procedures, get loads of rest, you know the drill."

"That you're a doctor with a busy and demanding life? Yeah, I think I do."

They smiled wide at each other again, standing there forehead to forehead, his hands warm and resting on her hips. "So dinner tomorrow?"

"Yes. I'd like that."

He kissed her once again, a quick parting kiss, but it was enough to send a flutter through her stomach. "Great. See you tomorrow."

As he walked away and she let herself into the building compound, she dealt with the warm and fuzzy feeling in her veins. Somehow, him laying down the rules had freed her. It might be okay to tiptoe into something with him. Who knew what could happen?

Because it turned out that she really liked that wounded warrior, Jackson Ryland Hilstead the Third.

For the next couple of weeks they kept their word and enjoyed each other's company at work and after hours several times, even spending the entirety of the last two Sunday afternoons kicking around together. Who knew running errands could be such fun? But because of what Jackson had proposed with their dating, and what she'd said about not being ready, they didn't sleep together. Never even came close. The amazing thing was, Jackson still wanted to hang out with her.

People at work began to catch on, giving knowing glances or making little comments to Charlotte. "I see you and Jackson are getting along." And "Was that you I saw having lunch with Dr. Hilstead for the third time this week?"

"You want to tell me what's going on?" The last remark came from Antwan Dupree. "Because I'm warning you, Dr. Hilstead is only trying you out for fun. If I were you I'd be careful not to get hurt."

"It's none of your business what I do." Was he for real? He'd come in here searching for a pathology report and had decided to lecture her on watching out for big bad wolves? He was the only wolf she knew. "Now, which specimen are you looking for a report on?"

He touched her arm, which in her book was a no-no, and she recoiled. "What I'm saying," he went on, unaware of how he'd turned her off already, "is that I'm for real." His cell phone went off and he took the call, having the nerve to carry out a brief conversation with "Baby," probably his current main squeeze, some OR nurse who didn't know any better. "I'll call you later, baby." He hung up, looked all earnestly at Charlotte and smiled.

The amazement on her face had nothing to do with his self-described—in her mind imaginary—charm. Check that. The appalled expression on her face. Did he have a clue about himself? She rolled her eyes in as big and overdone an arc as she could possibly manage to get her point across, in case Dr. Dense hadn't figured it out yet. "Mind your own business."

"I'm looking out for you, Charlotte. I'm just saying the guy's playing you. He'll drop you when he's done. Watch out."

"Your MO doesn't apply to every man, Antwan. Do me a favor and butt out of my personal life. It has nothing to do with you."

She gave him a quick report on the patient he was asking about and sent him on his way. But damn if her private insecurities about her body image hadn't flared up, letting the seed of doubt Antwan had planted about Jackson catch her off guard.

Yes, she did have continuing issues about believing any man would still want her once he discovered the truth. But Jackson seemed as reluctant as she was to take the next step. The truth was that over the last two weeks their make-out sessions had heated up and she wasn't sure how much longer it would be before she ripped off his clothes.

The attraction was definitely there for Jackson, too, if she judged rightly about certain body parts of his that had started becoming obvious in the last couple of kissing marathons. Wow. She longed to touch him, to feel the strength, the heat, but that would be playing with fire.

The man turned her on, often sending her home heated up and unfulfilled. How long could they keep this up?

She thought about him at night in bed, too, often imagining his sturdy body covering hers. Sometimes she'd touch her chest, running her palm across her scars, wondering what he'd think. Sometimes she'd fuel the fire of her imagination and let herself think about how it would be to feel him inside, bucking under him, or on top of him, taking him all in. How would he want to take her?

She was still a woman. Her breasts didn't define her. Her soul made her a woman. Would Jackson be able to get past her missing breasts and feel her soul if they ever made love?

She feared the answer, yet she imagined him panting on top of her; she dreamed about taking his weight and wrapping her legs around his hips so he could plant himself deeper inside.

Oh, yeah, she definitely wanted to rip off the man's clothes.

But the thought of the other half of that "ripping his clothes off" scenario—him seeing her completely naked—always sent her mind into a tailspin.

CHAPTER FIVE

JACKSON GRABBED THE pile of mail from his locked box at the condo building entrance and carried it into his apartment. It had been another long week, but spending a few evenings with Charlotte, plus looking forward to hanging out with her on Sunday afternoon, had made the grueling week completely tolerable. What more could he ask? He had a woman with a pretty face and an intelligent mind to look forward to being with soon. Actually, there was something more he'd like...

He shuffled through the mail, discovering an obvious—by the embossed gold foil envelope—wedding invitation from his cousin Kiefer. Aunt Maggie, his mother's sister, must be out-of-her-head happy. Then he thought of his own mother, who may have lost faith in him, and his mood shifted. He should call her more often.

The wedding was six weeks away in Savannah at Tybee Lighthouse. Hell, how many summers had he spent at the family beach house on Tybee? Too many to recall. Everyone had pretended not to mind the hot, sticky humidity while taking relief in the Atlantic Ocean. Mosquito-infested barbecues. Frantic capture-the-flag games after dark, which had inevitably turned into hide-and-seek scare fests. A smile crossed his lips again, remembering his younger cousin looking up to him like he was a god at fourteen. In fact, he sometimes wondered if Kiefer may have gone into medicine because of him. He sighed. Yeah, he had fallen far from that "god" title over the last couple of decades.

For one brief moment, a whimsical "what the hell" thought about going to the wedding and inviting Charlotte to be his guest nearly had him filling out the RSVP. Then reality forced him to think of the repercussions. His ex-wife, being a lifelong friend with his extended family, would most likely be invited. Having to face Evaline after a year, her still angry and feeling self-righteous. Facing his parents, Georgina and Jackson, the man he was named after. What about his still alert and oriented grandfather Jackson Ryland Hilstead the First? He'd be there, and so would the rest of his family.

How would it be to see them all again after leaving on such bad terms a year ago? It would be tough, for sure. To be honest, he didn't know if he was ready to handle it yet. Plus he didn't want his personal family drama to take away from Kiefer and…he glanced at the invitation to check the other name…Ashley's wedding.

His older son, Andrew, had sided with his mother. How much poison had she filled Andrew's head with concerning him? He understood—he hadn't been around as much as he should have when Andrew had been young. He'd failed him in that regard. But Andrew had zero empathy about his father falling apart from PTSD after his last army medical mission to Afghanistan, instead going along with his mother's opinion, insisting the loss of his leg had been his own fault for volunteering to go. Voluntary amputation, were they serious? The thought still hurt and angered him.

Jackson understood he'd scared people when he'd lost his grip on what was good and true and solid in life for those several months, but to blame him for losing a limb? He shook his head. At least he was making progress with Evan. Following him to Southern California had been the right move all around.

He set the invitation aside, not willing to say yes or no right away. Maybe he and Evan could make the trip together, and his son might act as Jackson's olive branch. He didn't want to write off all his relatives, but feared they may have already done the same to him.

Not wanting to slip into a funk over a simple wedding invitation, he thought about the gift of Charlotte. He'd practically blown any chance of getting to know her better on their first date, but she'd refused to be scared off by him. Hell, she'd even laid down a few rules of her own. He smiled at the memory. Spending time with a woman he liked and respected on so many levels had done wonders for his mental blues. She knew about his leg and it didn't seem to bother her in the least. Who'd have thought a pathologist would turn out to be warm and caring, not to mention easy on the eye? Now he grinned. She'd call him out in a heartbeat about painting all pathologists with such a broad brush. And that was what he liked about her, too. She didn't take his baloney.

Their make-out sessions had taken kissing to a new degree. Charlotte was responsive in every way, yet he sensed he couldn't cross an unspoken line, and so far he hadn't. As for him, he was definitely hot, bothered and ready for the next step. Sex! But Charlotte had been straight about taking their time the night he'd so brazenly laid out his terms for dating. *Don't dare think about marriage or kids.* As though he thought she'd been chomping at the bit to do just that. Maybe surgeons did have extra-big egos. So far she hadn't given any clear signals of change on the up close and personal level. He sensed something very private held her back, and he, of all people, needed to be understanding about that. But they'd been dating several weeks now and his dreams were growing more erotic by the night. Did taking things slow mean never?

There really was nothing worse than being

forty-two, a father of two grown sons, an established surgeon, having a career that for the most part he could be proud of, still being well respected by his peers overall, and horny. Horny as hell.

He headed to the kitchen to grab a soda and digest the current state of his life. Wedding invitation. Possible trip back home. New woman. No sex. Yet. Maybe, if he remained patient, something about that last part might change.

Or was it time for him to take the lead?

Charlotte rushed to the skilled nursing facility where Dr. Gordon had been staying during his continued oncology care. She'd heard he'd be transferred off-site to another, smaller, extended care facility, which meant she wouldn't be able to pop in so easily anymore. They'd kept him far longer than usual in the hospital because the chemo barrage had wiped out his T-cell count, making him a sitting duck for infection and nearly killing him. He was stable now, staff member status granted, and they couldn't justify treating him as an inpatient any longer. She wanted to be there for him during this trying time, since his wife, Elly, had passed away and his son lived out of state.

When she arrived at his bedside, she found him smiling, which surprised her. Word was his treatment hadn't got the results the doctors had hoped for. Surely an intuitive and bright man like James Gordon knew the downward course of his prognosis?

"Hi." She tried her best to sound casual.

His milky eyes brightened at seeing her. "Hi, dear." Dr. Gordon had started calling her "dear" and the honor nearly tore her heart every time she heard it.

"So they're moving you to some swanky 'let's pretend this isn't a hospital' kind of place, I hear."

He chuckled. "Yeah, kind of like that place all the old actors go to die."

She flinched. "Please don't say that."

"Don't get your knickers in a twist, kiddo. I'm just being funny. You know my motto—life isn't about what might happen, it's about what's happening right here and now. Today I move. Personally, I fought with them, told them I can take care of myself. I don't see why I can't go home."

He was getting frailer by the day, and she'd heard he'd had a fall once and had almost fallen a second time but a staff member had caught him. If he were left on his own, he could wind up breaking something and making his situation worse.

"The bastards—pardon my French, but the medical insurance department ticks me off—say twenty-four-hour in-home care costs too much. I know they're lying. Hell, I'd even pay for it. I get I'm a risk to myself." He shrugged his bony shoulders. "So, I go, and I bid thee adieu." He touched his forehead as if lifting a cap.

She shook her head. "No. You can't say goodbye to me. I'm coming to see you at least twice a week."

"My dear Charlotte. The thing for you to know is I'm feeling good, no more fevers, and I continue to have high hopes of beating this blasted cancer. As crazy as it sounds, coming from a pathologist, I've decided to remain optimistic, to let my natural human spirit overtake the practical scientist inside. If they want to extend the treatment and move me to a smaller, cheaper medical facility, fine, I'll go. The only thing I resent is not having any say in the matter."

She wished she could take her mentor home with her—that she could request a leave of absence to care for him—but her job was to keep his department running and that, at least, could give him peace of mind. She held his hand and they sat quietly for a few moments until someone appeared at the door.

It was Jackson, and even now, after all the time they'd spent together, the sight of him made her pulse do a loop-de-loop.

"I wanted to come and say good-bye before they rushed you out of here. Damn hospital budget and all," he said.

"Yes," Dr. Gordon said. "You being a lowly staff surgeon wouldn't have an iota of clout, would you?"

They laughed together, Jackson being better at getting when a man was trying to be funny than she was. She could see past the thin facade of tough-guy banter, how Jackson cared for

James, and the respect was mutual. The knowledge landed like a splat of thick, gooey warmth on her chest.

For the next several minutes they all sat around and chatted about anything and everything other than James's condition or his move. Which meant good old hospital gossip, the kind doctors enjoyed just as much as any other employees. Though Jackson did suggest there might be a good-looking nurse to ogle where he was going. That got a laugh, too. "I'm old but I'm not dead," he insisted. If there was such a nurse, he'd notice. He also wanted to know all about the pathology department, and had some suggestions for issues Charlotte had brought up before. She could tell he needed to feel useful, and she'd make sure he still knew how much he was needed as her mentor.

Two patient transfer attendants, a young man and woman, arrived in his room, and Charlotte and Jackson stepped aside as they packed up what little of James's personal effects were there, then got him on their gurney and carted him off to the waiting ambulance.

Charlotte and Jackson followed closely along

until they were outside. She didn't care if it was inappropriate or not—she kissed James on the forehead and gave him a hearty hug before they could slide him inside. "I'll be in touch soon."

"I'll hold you to that." He patted her arm and she could tell he bit back a lot of emotion, so she stepped away to make it a little easier for him. And her. Soon the ambulance doors were closed and all she could see of her mentor was his chemo-ridden head with just a few remaining wisps of white hair through the small back windows. Her heart clutched and her eyes stung.

Once the ambulance had driven away, she let go of her tears. Jackson's warm grip on her shoulders gave her something to lean on. He turned her toward him and circled his arms around her. "You're a good friend to Jim."

"I think I've told you before he's my mentor, but in so many ways he's been a father to me these last few years."

"He's a good man."

"Yes. Just now he reminded me about something he says from time to time, and why I'd forgotten, I don't know. He said, 'Life shouldn't be about what might happen, it should be about what's happening right now.'"

The deep personal meaning of that statement, spoken the day she'd finally made her decision to have the radical surgery, plus the fact that James Gordon was the first and only doctor other than her personal surgeon to know, had made a deep impression on her. He'd told her that he didn't think she should spend her life worrying about getting the cancer that had killed her mother, and if the surgery could offer her peace of mind, then she should do it. Then he'd assured her she wasn't crazy for taking the matter into her own hands. Just now he'd admitted he wished he had more say in his own treatment, then just as quickly had told her he'd decided to remain optimistic about beating his cancer. His choice, and a good one.

"Sounds like a solid motto for a good life."

She nodded. "He blew me away, sounding so upbeat about his condition." She pulled back from his shoulder and looked up at him. "He said he's decided to be optimistic instead of thinking like a scientist. He intends to beat it from that angle."

Jackson squeezed her a tiny bit tighter. "Then let's do the same, be optimistic for him."

"Yes. That's good advice. My mother was hopeful until the very end. She was amazing." Oh, if she kept on with this line of thinking she'd be blue in no time.

"I've got an idea. What do you say we take a walk on the beach at Malibu? Then I'll take you to a funky but great little place Evan and I discovered a couple of weeks ago." Jackson must have read her mind about needing some serious distraction, and his suggestion sounded perfect.

"I'd love that, but isn't Friday your night with Evan?"

"He'll understand."

Before she could protest, Jackson had his cell phone in hand and speed-dialed his son. Because she needed and wanted his company, she didn't try to stop him.

"Oh," he said, returning the cell phone to his pocket and pulling something else from the other one, "I almost forgot this." He handed her a candy bar. Her favorite, a Nutty-Buddy. "This should keep your blood sugar up until we eat dinner."

"How sweet of you!" This simple gesture proved his thoughtfulness and touched her more than she cared to admit. "Thanks. And the best part is I know I don't have to share it with you."

First dropping her car off back home in Thousand Oaks, they took the Las Tunas Canyon route through Agoura to the Pacific Coast Highway, and made it to the beach with plenty of daylight left. They parked and kicked off their shoes and walked a long stretch of sand, holding hands and listening to the waves crashing against the shore, while they inhaled the thick salty ocean air. They held each other as the huge-looking golden sun slipped bit by bit over the horizon, and Charlotte couldn't remember a sunset she'd ever enjoyed more. Because she was watching it with Jackson.

Then, as promised, he took her to a trendy though decidedly funky little hole-in-the-wall for a vegetarian meal complemented by organic pinot gris. Whatever they had done to the "green" wine, it tasted so good Charlotte decided to have a second glass. Why not? Jackson was driving.

Jackson wasn't being forward, but after dinner Charlotte seemed to have just begun to relax, so instead of taking her home, where she'd immediately start fussing about his needs, he decided to take her to his condo. Who was he kidding, calling it a condo? It was more like a glorified apartment, but it served his purpose, and since it was in Westlake, it cost a pretty penny for the privilege of living there. Why not show her how a new bachelor lived?

"So here's my place," he said, switching on the lights in the living room. The curtains remained drawn along the sliding glass doors, and the air felt heavy, especially after being at the beach. He strode to the wall and pulled back the drapes then opened the sliders for fresh air, suddenly aware how nervous he felt, having her here. It was another warm and inviting early summer evening, without a trace of humidity, which always amazed him, and the light breeze quickly chased out the stuffy air. He inhaled, forcing himself to relax.

"Make yourself comfortable," he said, heading to the kitchen to open a bottle of wine. He hadn't ordered any with dinner, though Charlotte had raved about the organic "green" wine. His thoughts had been that tonight she needed to let go a little, and if enjoying a glass or two of wine was the way, he'd make sure she got home safely. He picked up two wineglasses by the stems and carried everything to the other room.

Charlotte had made herself comfortable on the small but functional gray linen upholstered couch overrun with brightly patterned pillows, which she'd pushed aside. The pillows were only there because that was how it had been displayed in the catalog. What did he know about decorating? That had always been Evaline's job. When he showed up back at the sofa, her amused expression changed to a wide smile. Combined with the light blush of someone who'd been enjoying her wine with dinner, the look was more than appealing. "You've been reading my mind a lot tonight," she said.

"I try." He opened the bottle of chilled chardonnay and poured them each half a glass. She sipped, and he joined her. "This is where I hang out when I'm not at the hospital." He wished he could read her mind a little more right now, but on the other hand, maybe he didn't want to know what had put that previously engaging gaze on her face. She was probably suppressing a laugh at his decorating skills, or lack thereof.

"Rented furniture?"

Okay. Maybe he had read her mind again. He dutifully nodded. Was it that obvious?

"Not bad, but it tells me you don't plan to stick around."

"I think I've told you that I came here to be near my son, and that was the extent of my plan. Oh, and then I found the job at St. Francis." He took another drink.

"And then you started showing up in my office." She quaffed more wine, looking self-assured. He liked it.

His eyes crinkled with another smile. The topic was starting to get good. Plus her attitude had taken a turn toward sassy. "That I did. There was a surprise beauty in that office."

He gave another half smile. She stared lightly at him. It made him think there was a lot going on inside her head right then.

"Did you have any idea how long I had a crush on you?"

So he'd been right about a lot going on behind that getting-more-relaxed-by-the-minute stare. "I thought *I* had a crush on *you*."

She sat sideways on the couch, one leg bent on the cushions, the other crossed over it. He faced her. With the tip of her now shoeless toe, she made contact with his knees. "I liked you from the first time I saw you, and I couldn't believe how interested you were in the slides."

"That's because I was interested in the person showing me the slides." He touched her, soon caressing her toes. She drank more wine, letting him have his way with her foot.

"I liked being in the dark with you, getting to test out whatever aftershave you threw on. You don't have a favorite, do you?"

He shook his head. Shrugged. He liked how she was opening up and he didn't want to stop her, so he kept quiet.

"I can remember the first time our knees touched. You inhaled and I thought it was so sexy. You realize how sexy you are, right?"

His brows shot up. This was really getting good.

"Uh, I hadn't thought about that in a long time."
Three years, to be exact. Since losing his leg.

"May I ask what happened to your marriage?"

Ah, damn, she'd pulled a quick one on him
and changed the topic to something much less
appealing, but Charlotte deserved to know the
whole story. His version anyway. And, more importantly, he'd reached a point where he knew he
could trust her with it. "Evaline was my high-
school sweetheart, and she followed me to college. We got married sooner than I had planned.
Actually, I wasn't even sure I was planning on
it, but she, or rather we, got pregnant and, well,
I did the right thing. We were parents at twenty-
one, right when I started med school." He took
a drink of wine, uncomfortable about reliving
his past.

"Obviously, I wasn't around much, which didn't
help things, but we muddled through. Two years
later, she got pregnant again. I have to admit I
was not happy. She'd stopped taking her birth
control pills and didn't bother to tell me." He took
another drink. "I'll be honest and say I kind of

felt like she'd trapped me. Not very heroic of me, but I'm being honest with you."

"I can understand that. No judgment here."

"Thanks. She was the first woman I loved and I held on to that, and we just kind of kept moving forward. But when I signed on for the army reserve medical unit and was away from home a lot, I'd come home and feel distant. That's when I realized our marriage was in trouble. The thing was, she liked being a doctor's wife, and I liked being a surgeon, so at least we had that in common."

He tried to make light of it and even forced a laugh, but he glanced at Charlotte and saw understanding and empathy on her face, not sympathy. At least that was how he needed to interpret it. She reached across the couch and squeezed his forearm. *Keep going*, she seemed to say. "Fast-forward to my coming home from a second tour to the Middle East, this one voluntary, missing part of my leg and a total mental mess, and, well, I fell apart, and she fell apart, and so did our marriage."

An old lump of pain started radiating smack in

the middle of his chest. He took a deep breath, feeling grateful to be here right now with Charlotte. He wondered about her, too. "And speaking of marriage, why isn't a fantastic woman like you married?"

Her brows lifted. She sipped from her glass, looking thoughtful. "I was engaged. I planned to have the American dream of a career, a husband, kids. We were all set for it, too. Then..." she slowly inhaled "...things changed." She stopped and looked at him. "Would you mind if we went back to talking about how much we like each other?"

So she didn't want to open up right now. Maybe it still hurt too much, and if anyone in the world could understand that, he could. "I'll start. Knowing I'll see you at work at some point every day makes me happy to wake up. I haven't felt anything like that in, well, a long, long time."

A sly smile crossed her full and kissable lips. "My turn?" He nodded, eager to hear what she'd have to say. "Your blue eyes are killers, and there's something about your almost curly hair that drives me wild."

He hoped she planned to come on to him because the compliments were making him hot. He took a draw from his wine then put down his glass on the nearby coffee table. Something told him if she kept on with this line of conversation, he might soon want the use of both hands.

"And you've been the highlight of my day more times than I can count. Even when I first started at St. Francis. There you were, sitting in the dark." He moved closer, took a lock of her thick brown hair and played with it. "You always seemed calm, maybe a little reserved, but it was a welcome change from all the type A personalities in my department. I always looked forward to seeing you. Always." He leaned forward, and having moved her hair away from her ear, he lightly kissed the shell. "I thought you were sexy but you didn't seem to know it, which made you all the more appealing." He nipped her earlobe then watched the flesh on her neck prickle. "Now that I know you better, you're driving me crazy."

She took a quick last sip of her wine and set the glass down. He couldn't help but get his hopes up that tonight might be the night. Soon after their gazes met and melded, planting a solid yes in his mind. He kissed her, pulling her closer. She settled into his arms and kissed more hungrily than usual. They were getting pretty damn good at this part. Making out. He deepened his kiss and a tiny moan caught in her throat. His me-man-you-woman switch clicked on and his needy hands roamed her shoulders and arms and soon slid over her waist and up to her breast.

She stiffened so noticeably he stopped kissing in order to look at her. This wasn't the first time it had happened. "Am I doing something wrong?" He spoke quietly, his version of tender. "If there's anything I need to change, tell me so I can fix it."

She shook her head, switching from the relaxed sensual compliment-giver of a few moments before to a cautious woman with glistening brown eyes. She glanced over his shoulder rather than look straight at him. A sense of dread seemed to hover around her. "You've heard me talk about my mother."

He nodded, and he knew the stats about breast

cancer, too. Was that what held her back in life? The fear of getting cancer?

"On top of having the strong family history, I have the Ki-67 blood marker *and* the BRCA1 and 2 gene mutations, plus SNPs—single nucleotide polymorphisms."

So that was the rest of the story, and a tough one to accept for sure.

"Not good. Right?"

Still considering the stark reality of what she'd just said, he didn't answer right away, but he had to agree. The odds were against her. "Is that what stops you from getting closer?" Would she never let him, or anyone, into her life because of that?

She took a deep jittery breath, shifted her gaze to his hand, touching his fingers, playing with them. Every time she touched him he responded, and soon their fingers were laced together, his thumb rubbing along the outline of her palm. She worried her mouth. "So two years ago I had preemptive surgery, bilateral radical mastectomies without reconstruction." She may as well have blurted out there was a monster in the house—the sudden news felt as jolting.

He gripped her hand tighter as the realization of what she was telling him registered. This beautiful young woman had had her breasts removed to avoid being diagnosed with cancer in the future. As a surgeon, he knew exactly what she meant. He knew what unreconstructed mastectomy scars looked like. Hell, he'd given those scars to hundreds of women over the years. But most opted to have implants along with the surgery. From several of his own patients who'd taken Charlotte's route, he knew the sorrow the women went through afterward. Dealing with body image was always the toughest issue. Yet her surgery had been voluntary, and she'd made the choice not to have reconstruction.

It also became clear why her engagement had ended. The guy hadn't been able to take it.

So the natural curves on display in her clothes were thanks to that special bra he recommended to his own patients. It sure had fooled him. Now he understood why she always tensed up when he started exploring that part of her body.

He needed to make it clear that he wasn't that guy, the guy who couldn't take it.

He pulled her hand to his mouth and kissed it, kissed each finger and the inside of her wrist. He just wanted to love her, to ease her fears, to let her know that, though, yes, he was shocked, it didn't matter to him. His other hand caressed her neck. "If you're worried what I might think, I'm going to quote back to you what you told me Dr. Gordon said. 'Life's got to be about what's happening right now, not about what might happen.' And right now I want more than anything to make love to you."

She leaned into his hand, and his thumb traced her jaw and earlobe. He pulled her to his mouth and kissed her again, a long warm and sensual message he hoped would get through to her. But he knew she needed to hear it from him, to make sure without a doubt he understood.

"You have no idea how much it meant to me when you didn't react over my leg. I didn't see the look of horror in your eyes that I've seen before. And, believe me, there's no hiding it if it's there. I've seen people try." He took both her hands in his and squeezed them. "Look at me." She complied and he gazed gently at her. "So, of all the people in the world, I know how it feels to be insecure about an imperfect body." He kissed her once more to prove his point, to hold her near, feel close to her again, hoping he was getting through. She seemed to welcome his kisses, as she always did. His hand slid to her shoulder and upper arm again, where he held her firmly.

"Charlotte, I've been fortunate enough to have lots of time to get to know you and you should know that I think you're a beautiful person both inside and out." A light ironic laugh puffed from his mouth. "Hell, I'm the perfect *imperfect* person to be with you tonight. But only if you want it." He could only hope his expression and invitation looked and sounded as sincere as he truly was.

Her hesitant, dark and worried eyes relaxed the slightest bit. Her hands moved to cup his cheeks as a look of deep gratitude crossed her face. Her fingers felt cold, nervous. But there was something more in that gaze, some kind of promise, or was it blatant desire, like he felt firing up again inside. She leaned forward and kissed him, lightly at first, then released all the passion she must have let build during his confession. Because that kiss soon morphed into a ravenous need to be close, to feel, to excite and take.

To make love with him.

CHAPTER SIX

JACKSON HOPPED OFF the couch and began searching through cabinets and drawers, leaving Charlotte confused. Had she turned him off? She'd
thought she'd been giving him all she had, sending the strongest message possible—*I trust you.
Take me, I'm yours!* She followed him into his
small kitchen. He looked over his shoulder, apparently clutching some stuff in his arms.

"My mom sent out a bunch of things that I
never thought I'd use in a hundred years, but
guess what." He turned, showing her his arm-
load of candles in various sizes and containers.
"Tonight is the night."

She laughed with him, then reached out and relieved his overloaded arms of a few of the candles
to help before he dropped something.

"What do you say we put these babies all
around the bedroom and..." now that he had a

free hand he pulled her close for a quick kiss "…light them up."

The fact he wanted to create some atmosphere for their first time being together made a powerful impact on her wavering mood. The gesture of using faint candlelight as a buffer hit her like the thud of a palm to the center of her chest. They were going to have sex tonight. He would see her naked. Rather than make a big deal out of it, and possibly make him self-conscious about his eagerness, she sniffed one of the candles, vanilla, then another, rose. "Things should smell pretty good, too." She gave her best shot at sounding anything but the way she really felt—nervous! "One more thing. I don't take birth control pills. I use a diaphragm, and I didn't bring it tonight."

He watched her for a second or two, understanding and tenderness like she'd never seen centered in his bright blue gaze. "I've got that covered." His sweet gesture calmed her jitters. "Follow me."

There was nothing quite like a man on a mission.

Once the candles were strategically placed

around his surprisingly spacious bedroom, she took a quick trip to the bathroom while he circled the room, lighting each one. Just before she exited she looked into the mirror. "Are you ready for this?" she whispered, her pulse quickening from her jangling nerves, her fingers slightly trembling. Then she noticed a subtle reminder, the crutches leaning in the corner. Jackson would need them without his prosthetic to get in and out of the shower. His prosthetic. She'd made full disclosure just now in his living room. A man who wore a prosthetic partial leg would understand.

She refused to let Derek's memory ruin the chance for something new. Something better. Tonight she'd trust her gut—which seemed to have turned into a butterfly farm—trust Jackson, and maybe finally turn the corner to wholeness. She took a deep, shaky breath and opened the door.

Jackson stood in the center of his room, several feet from the foot of his bed, surrounded by soft candle glow, looking more handsome than she'd ever dreamed. While she'd been in the bathroom and he'd been lighting candles, she noticed he'd also found a condom or two, which were now sitting on the bedside table next to a tall, wide white candle. A man of his word.

He smiled at her, candlelight dappling the deep creases on either side of his mouth, looking sexy as hell, and she walked toward him. He took her into his arms and held her still for a few beats of her heart. She let go, melted into him, loving his welcoming warmth. He kissed her temple and ear and she inhaled the trace of his spicy aftershave along with the swirling candle scents, a mixture of vanilla and rose. And magnolia? Lifting her chin, she met his lips and soon didn't have to think, since their kisses always took on a life of their own.

Out of breath from his greedy kisses, her hands landed on his chest and slowly unbuttoned his shirt, mostly because she was nervous and her fingers weren't cooperating with her desire to get that thing off him! Pulling open the shirt, she reaped the benefit of her effort, being treated to the smooth skin of his muscled shoulders and his impressive chest dusted with brown hair. Her fingers traced over the tickly feel of him before she kissed him there and there and finally at the notch at the base of his throat.

He let her undress him, unselfconsciously needing to sit down when she'd pulled his jeans to the hard prosthesis with its silicone suspension sleeve. The layered muscles of his runner's thighs and his washboard tight abdominals distracting her from that detail. The thought of removing the prosthetic had never entered her mind.

"This one is different," she said, refusing to avoid the obvious, besides the fact they wanted each other.

"It's my everyday leg, complete with shoe." He smiled with understanding over her question. "The one you saw was my sports version."

"The blade?"

Now he grinned. "Yeah, I'm a blade runner."

She returned his smile, but wanted him to understand she was only being curious. "So how do I take this off for you?"

After a moment's hesitation, probably considering that he'd never been asked that question by a woman he was about to have sex with before, he showed her the button to click down toward the prosthetic ankle joint. She followed his instructions, and he guided her on how to slide down the bulkier and harder version of leg. As she studied it, he quickly removed the liner with the pin that clicked into the joint down by the ankle. And that was that.

She glanced at what remained of his leg beneath his knee, the flesh and bone part, then quickly back to the rest of him. Choosing to focus on everything about him, and not just the one area he might be self-conscious about, she ran her hands along the length of his thighs and looked into his darkening eyes. She perfectly understood how he'd feel if she stared at the part that was missing.

He pulled her to him, kissing her again, bringing things back on track—they wanted each other—with his hands roaming all over her. His fingers found the hem of her cotton pullover, his intense gaze seeking hers for the okay. Would she make this revealing moment one to dread or, just like him, a matter of fact? She pecked his lips in answer, so he gingerly lifted her top, giving her time to adjust to what he planned to do next. But when he reached for one of her bra straps, her hand flew to his.

"That look of horror you described earlier?" she whispered. "I know what it is."

His gaze narrowed with concern.

"I was engaged when I had the surgery. We were going to get married and go for the whole package—careers, kids, the works. He didn't want me to have the surgery, but I insisted it was what I needed to do. And afterward he couldn't accept me. He just couldn't. He tried, but I saw it. He was horrified. I disgusted him. He pitied me. I—"

Jackson stopped her from saying another word by lifting her chin with a finger and delivering a tender kiss. As their lips pressed together and their tongues found each other, he undid her special mastectomy bra and removed it, never breaking from her mouth, instead deepening their kiss. He lay back on the bed and pulled her with him on top until her nearly flat chest was flush with his. Being this close to him, skin to skin, excited her. His warm, large hands explored her back and moved downward to her jeans, pushing them lower once she'd unzipped them, then cupping her bottom. With his palms firmly attached to her backside, she remembered how much she'd missed being explored by a man, and how good it felt now, loving this moment.

He concentrated on every part of her, rather than putting her missing breasts at the center. Finally, when she was completely naked with him, the fingers of one of his hands crossed her chest as lightly as a butterfly. The surprise of how sensual it felt to have someone else besides herself touch her there sent a blast of chills across her skin. Soon, while he continued to devour her mouth, his palm rubbed where her breasts used to be, and though many nerves had been severed during the surgery, his touch warmed and excited her as if her breasts were still there.

"You're beautiful," he whispered over her ear, and for that instant she believed him.

As their bodies tangled and tightened together, clearly turned on—her aroused and longing for more, him noticeably hard between them—she forgot about what was missing from him, and he obviously hadn't been turned off by her surgery. Maybe, she hoped, he'd meant what he'd said about finding her beautiful inside and out. Hadn't he just told her so?

He rolled her onto her back, pushing her hands above her head and kissing her chest in several spots. She could swear, in her mind, the nipples that were physically no longer there responded. His kisses traveled onward to her stomach, igniting more thrills, and worked their way over her hips and down across her thighs until his mouth settled where her heat mounted, tightened and balled into raw need. As his tongue found her tender folds and circled the tip of her sex, setting off amazing sensations bordering on lightning and fireworks, every worry and insecurity about her body image left her mind, to be replaced by one thought. At her core she was a woman and nothing could take that away.

A few minutes later, when he sheathed and entered her, working her into another frenzy under the spell of his strength and persistence, and surrounded by flickering candlelight, she dared to look into his eyes. They were already locked on her face. Watching each other under the grip of bliss was more intimate than anything she could imagine. And like that she let go and shattered the boundaries she'd put on herself because of her wounds, and from his frantic reaction was fairly sure he'd done the same. She needed him and wanted to please him, bucking beneath him, and his near growling moan proved she was on the right track.

He cupped her hips, she tightened her legs around his waist, he steadily upped the tempo, and they soon ascended to that beautiful intensity she'd almost forgotten, where he suspended her with near agonizing magic. Faster and stronger, he took her there. Until she was so tightly wound and overloaded with sensations she lost it and came deep, long and forcefully. He soon followed her and they tumbled through that paradise together, and she felt more complete as a woman than she ever had in her life.

On Saturday morning her muscles ached from their making great use of the condoms and candlelight, until all had burned out. By then so had she, and falling into Jackson's arms, immediately going to sleep, seemed surreal. His rented bed was surprisingly comfortable, or maybe it was the man in bed with her? When she woke, she glanced up at him. He was already awake and watching her, lightly playing with her hair.

"Hi," she said.

"Good morning." His hand grazed her shoulder and arm. "You like eggs? I'm starving."

"I love eggs. You cooking?"

He sat up. "You bet I am. I intend to impress the hell out of you, too."

"I think you've already done that."

His slow smile and darkening blue eyes relit the lingering warmth right where they'd left off last night. He kissed her to help it along, and soon the thought of sleeping in on a Saturday morning seemed far more appealing than any old home-cooked breakfast.

Later, when they'd managed to make it out of bed, he loaned her a T-shirt to wear with her underwear while he planned to dazzle her with his culinary skills. Before putting it on, out of habit she reached for her fully formed bra, but he stopped her.

"You don't need that around me." He ran his hand across her chest, up her neck and across her jaw, then kissed her. "I like you exactly the way you are."

CHAPTER SEVEN

AFTER CHARLOTTE AND Jackson's first night together, some wild, wanton woman had been released, a part of her she'd never before explored. Complicating things, she never knew when Jackson would pop in her office, his mere presence reminding her how much she wanted him. Usually his visits were after a particularly stressful surgery. He would drop in, close the door, and dance her into the corner to kiss her hard and thoroughly then make no excuses for how much he craved her. And she loved it! Then, with her feeling all hot and flustered, they'd promise to spend the night together, and that would be that.

This time, late on a Friday afternoon, it was the night he routinely had dinner and a movie with his son. With that one earlier exception, they never planned to see each other on Friday nights, so they'd have to put their lust on hold.

She'd worn a loose and flowing gypsy-style skirt to work, hoping he'd see it and compliment her. She loved his compliments.

When her lover came into her office and closed the door, he had a hungry look in his gaze. He took her hand and pulled her to him, kissing her, fingers digging into her hair, walking her backward to the wall, pressing her there. "Nice skirt," he said, playing with the fabric and just happening to find her hip and soon her bottom in the process.

In no time she had one thought on her mind and was totally grateful for her choice in skirts. Her leg lifted and attached to his hip, bringing his body flush with hers. Thanks to the thin fabric of his OR scrubs and her skirt, she felt nearly all of him as he stroked along her center. Wrapped up in the thrill of the moment, him igniting her and wreaking havoc with her good sense, she whispered, "Let's do it."

"You have no idea how much I want to." He kissed her roughly, slipped his hand between them and cupped her, moving up and down, fanning her fire nearly to the point of no return. He took a ragged inhalation to stop himself from going further. "But we could get fired, and I need this job," he reasoned. His hot breath tickled over her ear as she ignored his logical warning. "As much as I need you..."

"The department is practically empty," she interrupted. "Lock the door," she hissed, completely lost to him and the moment, and she meant it.

He gave her a questioning look and she nodded her undeniable consent. She saw the flash of heat in his eyes. He nipped her earlobe, then her lower lip. "I can't think straight around you."

With the oddest sensation, she'd have sworn she had nipples and they were tight and peaked with her longing to feel him inside her. "You do some pretty crazy things to me, too. Please," she begged, pushing her pelvis closer to him. "Lock the door."

It had never computed before how isolated her office was. Or the advantage of the other doctors routinely leaving early on Friday afternoons. She was at the end of a long row of offices in the basement of the pathology department. No-man's-land.

From having been with Jackson a dozen times before, she recognized the shift in his expression, his heavy-lidded stare. All resistance was gone. Her insides quivered, knowing what would happen next. "Just this once," he swore.

Lightning swift he locked the door and riffled through his wallet for a condom. They were back where they'd left off, his hand finding her secret places and working wonders, and when her powerful moment came she let him cover her mouth with his palm to stifle her response. The last thing they wanted to do was draw attention to what was going on in case anyone was within earshot. He loved watching her when she lost it. And just then, thanks to his skillful touch, she totally had.

Someone knocked on the door. "Charlotte, are you in there?" It was Antwan.

With Jackson's hand still over her mouth and tightening, her gaze shot toward the ceiling. *Really?* Of all the bad timing in the world.

Jackson removed his hand from her mouth and put one finger over his. *"Shh..."* She felt the sudden urge to laugh. This was ridiculous, and nothing she'd ever do! But her pulse hammered in her chest, more from what Jackson had just done to her than from Antwan's unwanted appearance. Though the risk of being caught having sex, well, partial sex, at work kept her heartbeat racing along.

"Has Dr. Johnson left for the day?" Dr. Dupree called down the hall.

"I don't think so," Latoya's distant voice answered from the reception area. "Dr. Hilstead came by. Maybe they went for coffee."

Antwan tried the door handle. The nerve!

They stared at each other, neither hardly breathing. She clutched Jackson's arms and squeezed tight, her mind flying in a thousand directions. What should they do? What would they say if they got caught? What would her mother think?

"Well, she's obviously gone." Finally, they heard footsteps going down the hall and Antwan's distant voice chatting up the young receptionist. "It sure feels dead around here."

Latoya gave the requisite laugh at his sorry attempt at a joke with the pathology reference.

"What are you still doing at work?" Antwan's

attention had shifted. Good. They talked more, but Charlotte had quit listening.

Jackson gave her a stern look. "This can't ever happen again."

Feeling out of control and pumped up by the excitement, she grabbed his scrub top and pulled him near, then delivered a ragged kiss. "You're right—this has got to stop. But first it's your turn."

"We're crazy to risk it," he whispered over her ear, his hot breath melting her and dissolving into a cascade of chills down and over her breasts.

She got busy giving all of her attention to him, admiring how firm he'd stayed through the close call. He gave his rendition of a ragged kiss, far more intense than hers, taking her breath away. His weight pushed against her, her leg lifted again, and when he'd secured her to the wall, she lifted the other, clutching his hips.

"We really shouldn't," he murmured.

Farther down the hall, in the histology lab, the late shift technician stopped and listened, wondering where those muffled rhythmic thuds on the wall were coming from.

* * *

On a Monday, Charlotte had a phone message that Dr. Gordon was moving again. It was from his son Ely. He said he'd taken leave from work to be with his father and that Dr. Gordon wanted him to notify her.

She'd just got back from a quick but fun lunch with Jackson. No sex involved. Who knew how great hospital cafeteria food could taste when you were totally into someone? Now her lunch turned to a lump in her gut at the news.

Dr. Gordon had regained a lot of strength, and three days ago when she'd last visited he had been as feisty as ever. Maybe he'd figured out a way to beat the system. She wondered if Ely had volunteered to come or if Dr. Gordon had manipulated the visit. She wouldn't dare consider that his health circumstances had directed the move home. Had Ely implied he was there for hospice care?

Before she could form another thought her cell rang. It was Jackson.

"I just heard Jim Gordon left the extended care

facility for home. Maybe we should go visit him this evening."

"I'm not sure if his family would want that, but I want to."

"I'll give a call, let you know."

"Thank you." She had a stack of slides fresh from histology to study from Saturday's surgeries, and though her heart and thoughts were with her mentor, out of respect for him she knew his department needed to carry on.

After work, Ely had given the okay for a visit, so Jackson drove as Charlotte let several scenarios play out in her thoughts, though she never expected the scene they found when they arrived.

Dr. Gordon was sitting in an obviously favorite chair, judging by the wear and tear on it, and how perfectly the man fit into it, too. He gave an ethereal smile, his skin ghostly white. "Hello, dear."

She bent to kiss him on the cheek, which felt warmer than he looked. "Did you have to pull some strings to move home?"

No longer a curmudgeon, his gaze more impish now, he smiled. "Ely and Sharon are staying with me for a while." He officially introduced

Charlotte to his son and daughter-in-law. "The hospital decided I was in as good hands here as there. At much less cost to them!"

"That's wonderful."

Ely was a younger version of his dad with thinner eyebrows, though a bit taller with a friendlier face, and personality-wise, probably thanks to his mother's input, less off-putting. He hovered around his father, and Sharon seemed to sense her father-in-law's every need. Beyond giving him all the care and attention he'd require over the next few weeks, they radiated something that couldn't be faked—love for him.

Knowing her mentor would be surrounded by family and seeing how at peace he seemed, being back home, helped ease her worry about the significance of the move. No one mentioned the term "hospice care," and there wasn't a sign of medical equipment in the living room. Charlotte hoped for the best.

"I've asked Jerry Roth to take over as department head," he said. "There'll be a memo going out tomorrow."

So much for hope. Her heart ached at the news and what it might imply.

"He'll do a great job," she said, trying to sound upbeat. Jerry was the logical replacement—though she hated thinking that word—being the second most senior in Pathology at St. Francis of the Valley. Even with her foolish hope lagging, she wanted to reassure Dr. Gordon about his choice. "He's been steady as a rock while you've been in the hospital." Sitting nearby, Jackson subtly took her hand and squeezed his support.

"When I come back, it'll only be part-time."

The emotional teeter-totter had her sitting straighter. "You're coming back?" She couldn't suppress her surprise and happy relief, and for a man who didn't do impish, she could have sworn he savored playing her.

"I've been officially deemed in remission." As much as it went against his nature, her mentor beamed. "Don't know how long it will hold, but I'm feeling stronger every day, and hopefully, with Sharon's healthy cooking and the company of my son and friends like you, I'll be back in shape in no time at all."

"That's fantastic news, Jim." Jackson spoke up, a sincere smile on his face.

"Thanks. I'm just being realistic about not taking on too much when I come back."

"Wise of you," Jackson said.

Elated, and grinning to prove it, except probably sending a mixed message with the tears that had simultaneously cropped up, Charlotte clapped her hands. "I can't wait."

"To be honest, I can't either. I need a purpose besides being a pincushion and lab rat."

After a long drawn-out hug, and Charlotte realizing that the move and their visit may have taxed Dr. Gordon, she decided it was time to leave. But first, remembering all the things she'd wished she'd said to her mother during her ordeal, before it was too late, in case she never got the chance, she sat on the ottoman where Dr. Gordon's feet rested. Having him captive, she looked into his eyes.

"It's been hard, not having my mentor around these last few weeks. I want you to know how much you've taught me and how special you are to me. How much I still need you." She took his bony hand. "I've kind of put you on a pedestal, sometimes wishing you'd been my dad." She glanced up at Ely, noticing his approving smile. "I'm a better doctor because of you, and since I can't exactly go around saying this at work, I want you to know I love you."

He tightened his frail grip in hers. "Thank you. You're very special to me, too. Now quit worrying about me. You know my motto: life shouldn't be about what might happen, it's—"

Ely and Sharon joined in on the last part of the phrase, clueing Charlotte in that it really was a saying he lived by. "It's about what's happening right here and now."

She studied the man in his comfy chair, back in the home he'd made with his wife of fifty years before she'd died, his son and daughter-in-law like bookends on either side of him. Him being there "right here and now" looked pretty darned sweet, so she said good night and they left.

Moved by the warm and squishy moment that had just occurred inside Dr. Gordon's house,

Jackson stopped Charlotte before they reached the car. "I've got a wedding to attend back home in Georgia next month, late August. Would you do me the honor of being my guest?"

Surprise registered in her eyes, and she didn't answer right away.

"I figure if Jim comes back on the job part-time, you should be able to take a few days off." He opened the car door and let her slip inside, then walked around and got in, still waiting for her answer but not quite ready to hear it. "Before you make your decision, let me just say it's because we've got really close and I was hoping you'd come with me. The truth is, I'd feel better confronting the mess I left behind with you at my side."

"I'd love to go."

It was his turn to be surprised, especially because of the poor excuse he'd given for wanting her there with him. As backup? What had he been thinking? "You would? I didn't mean to imply you'd be a crutch or anything."

"I understand."

"Really?" Over the last few weeks he'd grown

to know Charlotte's body as well as his own, and he marveled over that gift. Since they'd started dating, he knew her intelligence was both a source of challenge and comfort. They understood each other. Hell, he'd torn a page right out of Jim Gordon's rule book to help convince her to give him a chance: *Right here, right now. To hell with the future.* Her warm and loving attitude seemed a gift from heaven, yet she'd just dazzled him again by being so willing to step into his past without knowing how bad it could be.

"Yes. I'd love to go."

How much more proof did he need about how special she was? "Well, in that case, I think it's about time you met my son."

Charlotte snuggled into Jackson's arms in her bed after making love later that night. Being tall, it took a lot to make her feel petite, but his broad shoulders and long frame did just that. Now that her personal shock of having a double mastectomy had barely made waves for him, often, when they were just staying in and hanging out, she'd walk around in a T-shirt or sweater without strapping on her bra, her chest as flat as his.

And it didn't faze him. He'd been the one to suggest it after the first time they'd been together. She considered that freedom a special gift from him. He really had proved to be the perfect *imperfect* man for her.

Just before she drifted off to sleep, one last thought crossed her mind: how life was looking up. Her mentor was in remission, the new guy in her life had just asked her to a wedding in his hometown, which proved he trusted her with a fragile part of his life. And now he wanted her to meet his son. She couldn't help but feel special. Yet he'd never come close to saying those three little words.

The big question was, was it safe to get her hopes up? Maybe he was just a guy like the rented furniture in his condo, temporary, useful for now, nothing to take for granted. He'd been very clear about never wanting to marry again or to have any more kids. Now that she knew the full story, she understood, too. He'd moved to California to be near his son, who would eventually graduate from college and move on. Why would Jackson stick around after that?

But right from the start, having laid down a few personal safety rules of her own for Jackson, like taking it slow before jumping into a physical relationship, she knew how easily a rule could be broken. Tonight that fact fed her hope.

Jackson was on his way out of the lunchtime surgical conference when he saw Dr. Dupree across the room. He'd had something on his mind and made a point to confront him.

"Dr. Hilstead. You need something?" Antwan was in the middle of sharing a recent conquest with a young resident.

"Yes, if you have a minute?"

The long-haired resident took the cue—in fact, looked relieved—and headed out of the auditorium with everyone else.

"I just wanted to let you know that Charlotte and I are a thing now, so you can step back."

"A thing?"

"Yeah, we're a thing."

"She knows this?"

"Most definitely. Anyway, you can step back now."

"Step back?"

"Yes, step back." Jackson emphasized the words for the guy who seemed to be playing dense.

"Sometimes ladies don't know what they're missing until they've tried it." His overconfident smile grated on Jackson's nerves. Was it a challenge? He also knew the jerk was referring to himself, Antwan, not Jackson, so he decided to spell it out for him.

"Trust me, she's tried it and liked it. I'm asking you nicely to leave her alone." Was he on the verge of flapping his arms and making monkey noises? *My territory. Leave!*

"If that's what she wants, fine."

Jackson stared at the dense doctor long and hard. But he didn't dare say the words that had just been planted front and center in his head. *She's mine.* That would make him feel a bit like he'd traveled back in time to a more dramatic stage, high school or college, when guys got all wrapped up in their women and proudly staked their claim. He was a mature adult now, in midlife, sophisticated and above getting into the fray. Yet feeling the intense need to make his point perfectly clear with a womanizing bozo like Dupree couldn't be denied, and it shocked him.

Where had that come from? What had happened to the civilized forty-two-year-old surgeon? He bit back the long list of things he'd like to say, deciding to go for terse. "It's what she wants. We want." Like he had the right to speak for Charlotte, as Antwan had already insinuated. But it was. It was what *he* wanted. And he was pretty sure she wanted it, too.

He turned to leave, deciding to let Antwan figure out for himself what that meant, thinking the Southern gentleman-turned-caveman was a welcome change. He'd just publicly admitted he and Charlotte were "a thing," whatever the hell that meant.

The revelation of admitting he had intense feelings again on *any* level, and in this case for someone else—for his lovely *Charlotte*—made him grin. He left the meeting feeling taller than when he'd arrived, though admittedly he glanced over his shoulder for any evidence of a feminist posse hot on his trail for daring to be the tiniest bit chauvinistic. That didn't stop him from grinning, though.

* * *

That Friday night, Evan turned out to be tall, like his father, with piercing blue eyes, but much fairer and with lighter, straighter hair. From this Charlotte deduced that Jackson's ex was a blonde. She let her insecure imagination go wild and envisioned a stereotypical image of a pretty petite Southern belle, a Georgia peach, as she'd heard it called. The thought made her cringe and hurt all over. But she'd thought about all she and Jackson had shared over the last several weeks, and how close they'd got. Then on the spot she decided it was better to be the extreme opposite from an ex—tall, olive-toned skin, dark hair and eyes, big-boned—than a dead ringer. Wasn't it?

Occasionally during dinner the strained dynamics between Evan and Jackson were evident, but only on certain topics, like the wedding and whether or not Evan planned to go. They agreed that Evan should fly out a few days early to spend time with his mother and brother, and as an observer the decision lifted a weight from Charlotte's heart.

Didn't they know that they had the same laugh?

A few times she had to double-check who had said what because they sounded so much alike, too. The kid was his son, there was no doubt, and they shared a lifetime together, well, Evan's lifetime, anyway. And she suspected the same would be true with the older son, the one who'd yet to offer Jackson a touch of grace. They shared genetic traits and familial similarities, and no matter how hard Andrew might try to ignore it, there was no way to forget it. Again, her heart ached for Jackson and his troubles.

As the evening moved on over tapas and beer at yet another trendy Westlake restaurant, Charlotte realized something important. When they talked about Evan's Bachelor of Arts major at Pepperdine, excitement radiated from the nineteen-year-old, and fatherly pride was obvious in Jackson's eyes, which were decidedly sexier and bluer than his son's. Then again, she was biased. She quickly figured how to keep the conversation focused on university and life dreams, and soon Evan seemed to see her as an ally instead of an adversary—the woman threatening to take his father away from him.

She made it clear how important she felt a well-rounded liberal arts degree was to send a person out into the world. Evan couldn't have agreed more. Jackson's endorsement may have come in delayed, but he finally chimed in.

After a couple of glasses of beer Charlotte let her truest thoughts slip out. "Thanks to science and extended longevity, what makes parents think their kids can know where their journey will lead at the ripe old age of nineteen?" Charlotte mused.

"Exactly!" Evan agreed. The look of appreciation she received from the young man nearly melted her heart. One day he'd have the world at his calling, but he needed to first figure out where he belonged. Pressuring him to make up his mind too soon would never help.

Then she glanced at Jackson, who didn't appear nearly as impressed with her statement as his son.

Evidently she'd hit a chord of contention between father and son, so she continued. "I mean, I know how I wanted to become a doctor at sixteen, and you, Jackson, probably had a similar experience, but not everyone knows for sure where they belong at such an early age. My sister tried going to college and discovered it wasn't for her. Now she's happy as a clam with three kids and running a family business."

She didn't want to imply that Evan should drop out, so she quickly added, "Getting a solid, well-rounded education seems like the best step forward for most. Right, Evan?"

Evan nodded.

"I want the best for my sons. If Evan is happy with his major, then I'm happy."

Charlotte believed Jackson, because of all the men she'd met in her life, he had proved to be honest and dependable, someone to trust, and these were three characteristics at the top of her "perfect man" list.

Before dinner was over Evan seemed to understand a little better where his father stood on his undergraduate degree choices, and Jackson had made extra points, proving he supported his son. Charlotte couldn't help but think maybe she'd had something to do with it.

Then, over dessert, the previously unspoken subject of Dad dating a new woman came up.

"So I guess you two are dating, right?" Evan said. "And you want my approval?"

Charlotte worked extra hard to not show her true reaction. *Yes, we're dating, but beyond that I don't know what's in store. Do we need your approval for that?*

Jackson glanced at Charlotte, she glanced back, and then he reached for her hand under the table. "Now that Mom and I are divorced, I hope you're okay with that."

"Hey, it's your life." Evan seemed to toss the answer a bit too quickly, maybe in an attempt to leave out the emotion behind it. Pain. "I mean, I know a lot's gone on with your war injury and PTSD and all, and things didn't work out between you and Mom, but, Dad, you're entitled to pick up your life and date again."

Jackson reached across the table and clutched his son's forearm. "You saying that means the world to me, Evan."

When they all said good night, Jackson gave Evan a bear hug, and Evan fully participated. The sight of the two of them hugging moved Charlotte nearly to tears, but she managed to keep her response in line, not wanting in any way to draw attention away from the big event of the night. Until, in true Southern charm fashion, Evan extended his hospitality to her and hugged her good night. As she hugged the bonier version of Jackson, managing to feel his sincerity, she couldn't help the moisture that sneaked over her lids.

"It was so great to meet you." She said it over-enthusiastically, completely different from the response she'd intended to give. Cool. In control. Sophisticated. *Really fun to meet you.*

Evan smiled and nodded, as though he was also surprised about how well the night had gone.

On the drive home, overall Charlotte thought the meeting had gone well and that Evan seemed okay with his dad moving on. At least she hoped Evan was being honest. Though the question still remained—where exactly was Jackson moving on to?

"What did you think?" Jackson asked.

"I think you've got a great son on your hands."

While driving, he flashed her a grateful and re-assured look. "I think you're right." Then, with his eyes back on the road, he added, "I'm really looking forward to the day Evan turns twenty-one and my job as parent will officially be over."

"Is that job ever 'officially' over?"

"The part about being completely responsible for them, yes. The being-a-parent part?" He grimaced. "Nope."

Now that the hurdle of meeting his son had come and gone, Charlotte focused on the next big event. Truth was, she'd interpreted the invitation to the wedding in Savannah as a turning point in their relationship. Though Jackson hadn't committed to the trip meaning anything beyond a few days together on his home turf. *With her as his backup.* Her thoughts, not his. She felt otherwise. He *needed* her there.

But if that was all he wanted, backup, she'd oblige. Because she knew exactly how she felt about him—this could be the start of something big! Old song or not, it was how she felt, yet she chose to hold her thoughts close to her heart rather than test the waters on Jackson. It was still too soon.

Two weeks before the big event she went shopping for a special dress. She whistled while she combed through the circular racks in the showroom, happily looking forward to visiting a state she'd never been to before. She loved it already since it was the place that had shaped Jackson into the wonderful, charming and sexy man she'd come to know and...and what? Was she there yet? Or was she stuck in the "start of something big" stage? Maybe she was waiting for him to catch up.

All the new and optimistic feelings ebbed when a wave of insecurity and anxiety took over and her stomach threatened to knot up and push out her lunch. She swallowed hard and forced herself to pull it together. Shocked by the emotional reaction the act of buying a special dress had caused—or was it thinking about feeling something more for Jackson than she'd ever expected?—she took pause.

Sure, Jackson had seen her and accepted her for who she was, but how would she measure up to the people back home? Wondering and fearing how she'd manage in a sea of people she didn't know, her only lifeline being Jackson, who would no doubt be dealing with a boatload of his own issues, she fretted. Suddenly depressed about her

tall and sometimes clunky-feeling appearance—
the hair that would probably frizz up in the summer Georgia humidity, not being able to buy a
perfect dress right off the rack, not to mention
a subtle competitive feeling toward his ex-wife,
which annoyed her to no end—she passed off
feeling out of sorts and generally unsettled on
nerves about the upcoming event. Not the other
way around—feeling profoundly sick to her
stomach on a perfectly fine Saturday morning,
and getting nervous about what it might mean.

Then she went back to hunting for that perfect
dress that would make her feel like a knockout.
A dress that would cause Jackson to see her in a
different light.

As a woman he couldn't live without.

CHAPTER EIGHT

ONE WEEK LATER Charlotte sat in the laboratory with one of the histologists assisting while she examined, described and cut sections from yesterday afternoon's surgeries and clinic procedures. This morning there were no less than twenty-five bottles of varying sizes, each prefilled with fixative. An appendix, a gallbladder with gallstones, a cervical conization, a large, dark and oddly shaped mole, a wedge resection of lung—removed by Dr. Jackson Hilstead, she noticed on the requisition, which meant he'd probably pop by tomorrow to look at the slide with her. That put a secret smile on her face. She'd been doing that a lot lately, smiling for no reason.

In walked Dr. Dupree, looking like he had something on his mind, and he immediately wiped her smile away.

"Haven't seen you in a while," she said, opening the first bottle. Not that she'd wanted to see him or anything. Oh, man, she hoped he didn't read anything into her off-the-cuff, trying-to-play-nice greeting. The man was incorrigible.

"I've been told to step back."

Well, it was about time someone did. Who, though—hospital administration, the sexual harassment team? She kept her smirk to herself. "Step back?"

Not wanting to let him slow her down on the job at hand, she examined, then interrupted Dupree to describe and measure the dimensions of a piece of tissue, then used a scalpel to find the best possible section to represent the entire specimen for slides and put it into a cassette.

He waited impatiently for her to finish. "Jackson said you two were a thing and I should step back. It was a couple of weeks ago, so I'm just checking if that's still true."

Her line of vision on the specimen flipped upward, catching her assistant's gaze, whose eyebrows nearly met his hairline.

Jackson had staked a claim on her? Glad she was wearing a mask, she hoped her smile didn't reach her eyes, though the thought of irking Dupree even more was tempting. "Maybe in your world 'things' only last a week or two, but I'm sorry to burst your bubble. The official word is, yes, we are still 'a thing.'"

Did you hear that, world? Why did that put an entirely new spin on the right here and right now and make her feel amazing?

The histology technician pretended not to be listening to every word as he labeled the cassette then placed it in a large buffered formalin-filled container in preparation for the overnight process. The next day, after cutting ultra-thin sections of the paraffin-encased specimens, the histologists would deliver a set of pink, blue and purple stained slides neatly laid out in cardboard containers for the pathologists to read.

This was tedious but necessary work, which took at least twenty-four hours to complete from the time of receiving the specimen to stained slides. Charlotte took her duty seriously and focused her attention on the specimens. Not Dr. Dupree. Even though what he'd said, not his visit, was responsible for her mood being lifted to one of elation. "If you'll excuse me, as you can see, I've got a lot of work to do."

Undaunted, Antwan waited for her to look at him. "I'll check back in a couple more weeks." And off he went.

The nerve of that guy. She huffed and the assistant shook his head. Yeah, they were on the same page about Antwan Dupree's reputation around the hospital. But beyond agreeing the guy was an idiot, no one could possibly understand where she was, in the condition she might be in, at this exact moment. She was on her own with that.

The room had special ventilation to suck out the caustic fumes, and she wore a duck-billed mask as well as a clear face guard to protect from any formalin splash into the eyes. It was the same thing she did on any given day at work without any side effects. Yet today, during the cutting process, she felt decidedly nauseous.

Who was she kidding? It wasn't just today.

Dreading what a week of all-day queasiness might mean, she promised to take a test once she finished the morning's lab work. She couldn't push it out of her mind another second.

At noon Charlotte stole away to the hospital laboratory and had a trusted and super-skilled lab tech draw her blood, barely feeling the prick of the needle. Then all she could do was wait for the result with fingers tightly crossed it would be negative. She couldn't let her mind venture into the realm of what she'd do if the pregnancy test was positive.

Absurd. She couldn't possibly be…could she?

As a resident pathologist, she'd seen and examined far more than her share of young women who'd wound up in the morgue, only to discover at the autopsy they'd died from blood clots related to their birth control pills. The clots may have lodged in their lungs or brain but, wherever they were, they'd wound up being the cause of death on the autopsy report. She'd stopped taking BC pills and, even knowing the odds of forming clots were extremely small, had chosen never to use them again.

So she'd been using a diaphragm with Jackson…except on that first night when he'd caught her by surprise and he'd used a condom. And that time in her office.

Later, with zero appetite, she forced herself to eat some lunch in her office when halfway through the intercom buzzer went off.

"Dr. Johnson? This is Sara from the lab. Um, your test is positive."

"Positive?" Had she heard right? Her heart tapped a quick erratic pace at those four little words. Her blood test was positive. She forgot to breathe.

"Dr. Johnson?"

"Yes, Sara, okay. Thanks." She'd done the worst job in the world of pretending she wasn't stunned. It seemed her little "thing" with Jackson, to use Dr. Dupree's term, had just turned into something much bigger. She was pregnant. No. No. *No.*

She hung up, reached for her trash can, bent over and lost the contents of her stomach into it. She was pregnant.

When she recovered, and was positive her voice wouldn't quiver, she picked up the phone and dialed Jerry Roth. "I'm not feeling well, just threw up. I'll need to take the afternoon off."

Since she was notoriously healthy and hardly

ever called in sick, he didn't hesitate to let her go. "Go. Take care. Feel better." If it were only that easy.

Once at her town house, having been suspended in a bubble of disbelief so she could drive home safely but now feeling numb, she got out of her clothes and into her pajamas. Why she decided it was the right thing to do she didn't know. But it was. Even though it was early afternoon and summer, she wanted—no, needed—to snuggle into her soft bathrobe, to hide out and hope to find comfort there. Then she made a cup of herbal tea, noticing a fine tremor in her hand as she dipped the bag into the steaming water.

One little blood test had, once again, turned her life upside down.

What was she going to do? She didn't dare tell Jackson until she'd made her decision. The man had been adamant about never wanting another child. He'd warned her on their first date, hadn't he, almost coming off as fanatical about it. *No more children.* If she hadn't already made up her mind about liking him by then, he would have chased her away with his proclamations. Even though the "no kids" rule had matched her own.

The night they'd first made love he'd opened up and admitted feeling trapped into marriage by his ex-wife. Not that she wanted to get married to him because she was pregnant. But right from the start he'd made it known he was off the market in the marriage department. She wouldn't do that to him. But the baby. What about the baby?

Out of nowhere a long-forgotten dream from before she'd learned about her genetic markers whooshed through her. Her once-upon-a-time hopes of having it all—marriage, a career, *children*. She'd loved her rotation through pediatrics in medical school. Yes, she'd wanted children. Little knockoffs of her and whoever her husband turned out to be. Warm and lively little bodies that hugged better than anyone else on earth. The only munchkins in the world who would call her Mommy.

She plopped onto her couch and hunkered down for an afternoon of soul-searching with a potential life-changing outcome. Who was she kidding? Her life had already changed that first morning in the dress shop with that odd sensation of illness that she'd brushed off as anxiety. She just hadn't known it yet.

Was there a scientific way to handle the situation? She'd already done the math and come to the conclusion the risk for her getting cancer was too high, so she'd had the operation. She also knew without a doubt she never wanted to pass it on. Now, though, she couldn't remember what the exact percentage was for a potential "daughter" to inherit her markers and gene mutations. A lot had to do with the father, didn't it?

She dropped her head into her hands, her thoughts fogging up, and stared at the teacup on the table in front of the couch. Besides being addled by nausea, her mind was fuzzy around the edges with waxing and waning emotions of fear and joy. She couldn't ignore the joy part, keeping her thoroughly confused. What in the world was she supposed to do?

She'd sworn since she'd discovered she had not only the breast cancer blood marker but also the gene mutation, hell, she'd been adamant about it, *never* to have a baby. No baby. No how. Any baby. Ever.

She remembered the day she'd begged her sister, Cynthia, to get tested and how she'd refused. Cynthia had already had a child by then—a boy—so at least that was one less concern for Charlotte. But when her sister had informed her that she and her husband were planning to try for another, Charlotte had stepped up her campaign. Finally Cynthia had relented and had tested negative. Charlotte had had to bite back her envy in shame. Of course she was happy for her sister, who'd gone on to have twins, one of whom was a girl, and she still worried about little Annie's future. Cynthia had the same parents yet didn't carry the markers. Where did that leave Charlotte, the bearer of the unlucky genes? Where would it leave her baby if it was a girl?

Though what she carried would only potentially affect a girl baby, for personal ethical reasons she could never take a chance, get pregnant and wait to find out the sex before making a decision. No way would she be a designer parent, picking and choosing the child's gender, so she'd accepted it would be better to never have children. At all.

So here she was.

She needed another cup of tea. Maybe a gallon of it.

Somewhere during the course of cup after cup of calming chamomile, her anxiety rose, and several visits to the bathroom later, cautious excitement tiptoed into the mix of out-of-control feelings.

What? How could she be excited about something she'd sworn she didn't want? A baby.

Well, because she'd never *actually* been pregnant before. And now that she was, it seemed like a quiet miracle. A gift she'd never expected but somewhere deep inside had still always wanted. A bubble of joy insisted on making itself known. For a few seconds Charlotte let herself feel it, float on it, dream with that joy. A baby. *I'm going to be a mother!* Say it out loud. Make it real. She whispered it. "I'm going to be a mother."

Oh, God, she needed to hug that toilet again.

A little later, groaning and lying flat on her back on the cold tile of the bathroom floor, she stared at the white ceiling and remembered Dr. Gordon's words—*Life shouldn't be about what* might *happen, but about what's happening* right now.

She'd been born with a genetic marker she'd had no clue about, had been a happy kid as far as she remembered, and a typical teenager, until her mother had got sick. Long afterward, she'd discovered her potential for cancer, something that could be measured and planned for, unlike most people who never knew or suspected anything until they got their diagnosis. She'd dealt with it in her own way, and now she had to search her soul to decide whether or not to allow that same chance for her baby because *life shouldn't be about what might happen.* The key word jumping out at her this time—life.

Right here and now a baby was taking form in her womb, and cells were dividing and multiplying at the speed of light. Amazing. A million things could change during the process of a pregnancy. The possibilities of "what might happen" were exponential. Extraordinary. But right this second it was a fact—she was pregnant. And it seemed amazing! But the scientific part of her brain sneaked back in. Yes, she was going to be a mother. Unless a long list of potentialities stopped the process. Most importantly, would she be able to live with the guilt if her baby turned out to be a girl and also carried the same genetic markers? Or the guilt of not letting her baby have a life at all?

Her head started spinning with overwhelming thoughts. Could a person overdose on chamomile?

She rolled onto her knees, stood and staggered to her room and her bed.

At this exact moment in time she, without a doubt, knew one thing and one thing alone—that she needed a nap.

The flaw with allowing herself to succumb to a long escapist nap—in this case several hours— in the late afternoon was having to lie awake with a gazillion thoughts winging through her head now, late at night. She couldn't get Jackson out of her mind. Of course. Every rule he'd laid down from the start. In spite of that, how wonderful and compassionate he'd turned out to be. What a great lover he was, how the thought of being with him always made her quiver inside. How he'd recently admitted to people other than her that they were "a thing," both at work with Dupree and his personal life with Evan. Hell, the whole hospital knew!

How he never wanted to get married again or have children.

Yeah, that part. Plus the fact his ex-wife had got pregnant and rushed him into marriage. There was that fear again—would he suspect her of trying to do the same thing?

She had to make sure he understood that wasn't her plan. Hell, she still had to wrap her brain around the pregnancy part. She was nowhere near ready to think about the concept of marriage.

Besides, he'd yet to tell her he loved her. A fact. Did she love him? If she ever married it would have to be for love, not because she'd felt forced into it. Nothing else would do.

What was she supposed to do about their relationship now that she was pregnant? Should she wait until after the wedding to tell him? Could she bear to be around him keeping such a life-altering secret, forcing a pretend face that communicated all was well, and, oh, hey, I'm having such fun, when in reality, since the wedding in Georgia was only a week away, she'd probably still be fighting morning sickness?

Would it be fair? To either of them?

She glanced at the clock. It was nearly midnight. Maybe he'd tried to call her this afternoon while she'd been passed out in a pregnant-lady stupor. She walked to the living room and found her purse. Sure enough, he'd called, not once but twice, and had left a message after each one.

"What's up? Where are you? I heard you left work sick. Can I bring you anything?"

And an hour later.

"So you must be feeling really crappy and you're sleeping, because I checked the hospital and you hadn't been admitted. Kidding, but not really. I'm kinda worried. Call me if you need me. Okay? I'm home."

The man deserved to know. Right here. Right now. She understood the bomb she was about to drop on him would probably— Who was she kidding about *probably*? It *undeniably* would jeopardize their relationship. Though the thought already broke her heart. She grabbed an already used tissue from the coffee table. He may only see what they had as a "thing," but for her he was the "start of something big" romance, the first man she'd trusted since Derek. For Charlotte trust was the step just before...

That didn't matter since it was probably all over now, and she owed him the truth. The man who couldn't wait for his youngest son to turn twenty-one so he'd be relieved of full-time parenting wouldn't want to start over again.

Making the call wouldn't be so scary if, in all the times they'd made love, he'd just once whispered that he loved her. She'd been foolish enough to hope he would, even while knowing it was too early for a declaration like that. Now, since the probability of him breaking things off was huge, and she'd never get the chance to hear those words from him, she had to prepare for the worst. She used that tissue again, wiping her eyes and nose. Would she ever hear "I love you" again? From anyone? *Stop thinking about what may or may not happen, get on with right here and now.*

One thing she knew without a doubt: telling a man something as monumental as this needed to be done face-to-face. Too much could be hidden over the phone. With the news she was about to lay on him she needed to see his eyes, to see his sincere reaction. And he needed to see how important this change in life plan was for her.

Her insides quivered, and it had nothing to do with feeling nauseous.

With trepidation she speed-dialed his number, making a snap decision to do something completely out of character, to lead with her feelings. Tell him how she really felt about him. Could she admit she loved him, or would it feel forced right now? Then, definitely, she'd have to get around to the other part of the issue. Or maybe she should feel him out first, to see how he felt about *her*. Oh, hell, nope. It was her call. Her "situation," and she should be the one to be boldly honest. She might not be able to say "I love you" yet, but she sure as heck had other feelings about Jackson.

An unexpected sense of hope took hold as his phone rang. *I know what I'm going to say. But the instant I hang up I need to jump into the shower and clean up because...man, oh, man... I'm a mess and he cannot see me like this when I break the news.*

Jackson stirred from a restless sleep and looked at the time. It was midnight. And Charlotte was calling. He hoped she wasn't horribly sick. He'd left those messages, asking her to let him know if there was anything he could do. He'd even considered stopping by on his way home from work. But knowing how independent she was, he'd opted to wait to be invited. On alert, he sat up and answered the phone.

"Are you okay?"

"I'm crazy about you."

"What?"

"I've been meaning to tell you how crazy I am about you for some time now."

Was she dialing drunk? She was the most practical lady he'd ever met. Why would she call and blurt out such a thing unless...? Maybe she had a fever and was delirious.

"Will you come over?"

She'd just told him she was crazy about him, was probably a little tipsy, and now she'd asked him to come over. With all the possibilities that proposition held, how could he refuse?

"I'll be right there."

As he cleaned up and got dressed, an odd thought about the midnight invitation to his lady's house made him smile. Plus she'd said she was crazy about him, which was totally out of character but made him feel like a prince. Who'd have ever guessed when he'd first noticed her all those months ago that the prim-looking and earnest-as-hell pathologist would have turned out to be a sexy drama queen? The funny thing was, he liked it. He *really* liked it.

Several other thoughts forced their way out of the recesses of his mind as he drove to her house. How Charlotte was healing him and how grateful he was for that. He'd been shedding layer after layer of protective defenses since he'd met her. Something about her had made him like her right off, but now that they'd got close—in fact, closer than he'd been to anyone other than his wife—it seemed he was becoming a new man. Because she'd made it okay. She accepted him. He felt things again. Life was something to look forward to, not simply to manage to get through day by day. And because of his changing, he thought about a future. Maybe right here in California.

Sometimes the way he and Charlotte got along made him wonder if he had ever really been close to his wife like that. Their hasty marriage hadn't felt like his idea. He hadn't felt nearly ready for it, or for becoming a father twice before he'd turned twenty-four. To everyone else, his family, hers, he'd been a young doctor with a bright future. They had been the perfect couple. So he'd learned to work that to his advantage. A wife and kids completed his package as a safe bet to hire into a respected surgical practice, to groom for bigger and better things, like taking on the role of department head of surgery at Savannah General. His stay-at-home wife had made it easy for him to shine, too. He was grateful for it. While he'd spent hours and hours working his way up, she'd raised the kids. Mostly alone. Especially after he'd signed on for the medical unit in the army reserves and had started volunteering for disaster missions. Had they ever been close?

Andrew and Evan had been the highlights of his life, though—he couldn't dispute that, even when working sixty-hour weeks and going away one weekend a month. He smiled as he sat at a red light, remembering the heat he'd taken from his grandfather for not strapping Andrew with the name of Jackson Ryland Hilstead the Fourth. Evaline had stood by him on that decision. He sure hoped Drew appreciated it. So his ex-wife had given him his family and had stuck with him until he'd fallen apart. What more could a man have asked?

For better or worse? For both legs? For a wife who wasn't repulsed by him? Someone to stand by him through the toughest trials in his life, not just the successes?

His smile dissolved. Those wishes required a lot in return. He'd let their relationship grow empty. Truth was, he hadn't been there for her beyond providing a home and a lifestyle loaded

with the perks of being the wife of a wealthy doctor. And that hadn't been enough. Because he
hadn't been around. For most of their marriage
that situation had been satisfactory for her. Until
he'd changed for the worse after taking that second tour in the Middle East in the army reserves
and had come home from Afghanistan.

Coming home a hot mess—to use his mother's
favorite saying—broken and disfigured. Coupled
with his PTSD and withdrawal, it hadn't been
nearly enough for her anymore. He'd stopped
being able to run a department. To do surgery!
The one thing he'd come to think was the reason
he'd been put on the planet.

Truth was, he hadn't been willing to fight for
Evaline like he supposed he should have. He'd hit
bottom so fast and hard his heart had splattered.
He hadn't had anything left. It made him wonder if he'd ever really loved her. Or vice versa.

So now he was forty-two, driving after midnight to a new woman's town house because she'd
dialed drunk, told him she was crazy about him
and invited him over. Crazy, right? But he was
excited about it. In fact, he hadn't felt excited

about much in life since the war injury…until Charlotte. The woman who was helping him heal step by step. He was a better man because of her.

And if her calling meant she wanted to take him to bed, hell, yeah, he was all for it. Even if her virus or whatever it was that had made her leave work got him sick, it would still be worth it. Because there was something close and tender they shared beyond the crazy-hot sex. It was called total acceptance, and that special part, her accepting him as he was, and him doing the same with her, was bringing him back to life. He could only hope she felt the same.

Charlotte's heart fluttered when the security light came on from the entrance gate. She hit the entry button to allow Jackson to pass and park, her lungs forgetting to breathe on their own. With damp palms she finger-combed her hair and took a quick glance in the hallway mirror. Did it really matter how she looked? Something far greater than her appearance was at stake.

He knocked, and she nearly lost her nerve.

Could she run to the bedroom and hide under her pillows?

Willing strength she wasn't sure she had, she bit her lower lip and opened the door. There stood Jackson in all his post-midnight glory. Hair dashingly disheveled, eyes bright and blue, huge questions in them. Late-night stubble. "You don't look sick to me. You look great." His expression was lusty and hopeful.

Her eyes closed as she inhaled before she could answer, picking up his fresh application of spiced aftershave and fighting a wave of nausea. "I'm not sick in the classic sense, though God knows I've been nauseous all day. Well, all week, actually."

He scrunched up his face, trying to follow her meandering explanation. With his high intelligence he was probably already putting the equation together. Or choosing to ignore it, in which case she'd have to hit him over the head with it.

"May I come in?"

Oh, God, she hadn't even let him inside. "Of course." She stepped back, but he reached for her arm and squeezed as he kissed her hello.

She flinched, but for one instant the gesture, his warm lips pressing against hers, calmed her. What would he think? Then her roiling nerves took over again. "Have a seat."

His glance seemed to ask, *Why so formal? What if I want to stick around and keep kissing you?* Yet he dutifully went to her beige couch and sat. "I get the impression you have something important to say."

Her eyes lifted to the ceiling. "That's an understatement." She halted any further comment from him by using her hands to tap the air. "Let me figure out how to best say this. Okay?"

"How to say what?"

She paced and glanced at him, could read confusion or irritation in his expression, or maybe it was concern. She was being too obtuse, and needed to get to the point of why she'd called him out in the middle of the night. He might really think it was just to have sex. She stopped walking and faced him, then took a deep breath, deciding to go full speed ahead.

"Okay, let me start from the beginning." She had his total attention and the responsibility seemed more than she could bear, but she forced herself to pull it together. She had no choice, so she blurted, "It seems I'm pregnant."

The words had the expected effect of hitting him like a brick. He didn't smile or jump up to hug her with joy. No, that was the fantasy version of how this conversation would go. Instead, his eyes flashed wide and his head jerked back. Far too authentic for her to handle right now. Apparently she'd left him speechless. So, with her feet planted, she opted to continue her story. "I never expected to be pregnant. I'm not trying to trick you into marriage or anything." She assumed he'd gone right to the conclusion that history was repeating itself all these years later. "I swear. But since you're the father, I owe it to you to be honest and up front." She stopped to swallow and take a breath. "I'm choosing to keep my baby."

And there it was, the horrified look, the you-blew-every-great-thing-we-had expression. The tension around his brows reminded her how he'd laid out the rules right from the start. He didn't want to get married. He never wanted to be a father again. Her insides clutched.

"I know. You don't want to be a father ever again. You made it very clear. And yet here I am telling you I want this baby. After swearing I never wanted to pass my cancer genes on to a child of mine." Her chin quivered, but she refused to let the emotions gathering speed inside take over, so she bit down hard on her lip and counted to three. "I am afraid and filled with guilt about my decision, guilt for you and for the baby, but I can't say I'm sorry. I just can't."

Finally, she had the nerve to look into his face and eyes again. True, at first he'd looked horrified, or that was how she'd read it, but now his mien seemed perplexed, as though he was trying to solve a mathematical problem. A very big and complicated mathematical problem.

She remembered the words he'd repeated to her before the first time they'd been together, and the more that she was getting used to being pregnant and dealing with it, she bent those words from Dr. Gordon and decided to toss them back at him.

"You were the one who quoted the good doctor that 'life shouldn't be about what might happen,' otherwise we never would have made love in the first place, right?'"

She suddenly had his undivided attention, the dumbfounded look nearly causing his mouth to drop open. She wanted to sit beside him and plead for him to understand, but she stayed right there, on the other side of the coffee table from him. "So that brings us back to what is happening right now. Yes, I'm pregnant."

"You're pregnant." Evidently he was still feeling stunned.

"Yes, and you made me that way." Her finger shot up. "No, that isn't exactly right. We got that way together. *We're* pregnant."

Still Jackson remained painfully silent. It cut like a blade through her center.

She'd just laid her fear, pride and guilt on the table and he wasn't rushing to save any of it. Her decision to stay pregnant seemed to be hanging in the balance of his grace. She couldn't allow him to have that control over her body and her baby. Could she stand to hear him tell her thanks but, no, thanks? Oh, God, no, it would hurt too much. Fear took over about what he might say, and as was her pattern of dealing with fear, she rushed into a response before he'd had time to digest her news and form the words for a reply. She simply couldn't take this agonizing pause. If he wasn't going to say anything right this instant, she needed to step in, take control, preempt the outcome. "Please, leave. Now."

"Charlotte." She heard pleading and frustration in the single word of her name.

She shook her head. "I promise not to upset your carefully planned-out life. I get it. You told me from the start. You've done the father-hood thing and never want to do it again. You're counting down the days until Evan turns twenty-one." Her fear seemed to change to anger from one breath to the next and she couldn't bite her tongue to stop the next thought from coming out. "I know you never want to get married again. Hell, you can be an old lonely man for all I care. I'm having this baby." Damn the break in her voice, the surge of hurt childishness, the threatening tears welling in her eyes. Damn them all. And damn him, too.

She scanned the table for more used tissues.

"Wait a second," he said. "You're reading all kinds of things into this, and I don't deserve your insults. Can you understand that I might need to digest everything you've just told me? You owe me a little time to think, don't you?" He stood, imploringly, it seemed, taking a couple of steps toward her.

She moved back. "Sure." She sounded terse.

Had she hoped for and maybe even expected too much from her Southern gentleman? He didn't rush to her or make a single promise. He'd simply stood there looking all befuddled. *You're what?* What he asked for was time. And a reasonable person would grant him that. But she was anything but reasonable in her pregnant and scared sightless state.

The saying that actions spoke louder than words hit her like a full frontal head butt, knocking her fear aside and fueling her anger. He obviously didn't want any responsibility for this baby growing second by second inside her. If he didn't want to jump on board with the pregnancy, that said all she needed to know, and so she didn't have time for him. If she were a princess, she would have him banished, but she was a modern woman dealing with a life-changing event, and it hurt to have to go through it alone, to not get from him the support that she'd secretly prayed for. Her secret dream. But so be it.

"Go," she said, trying to cover up her true feelings. "Think all you want. Nothing is changing on this end. Go. Go!" Had she actually yelled at him?

Because he didn't budge, she grabbed his hand, pulled and led him to her front door, and only because he was still stunned and didn't seem to have the ability to resist her did he allow her to push him out. Or maybe he wanted her to, to let him off the hook. *She kicked me out!* he could claim later—which only made her angrier. She closed the door with a bang, nearly in his face.

She wanted to cry and scream and drop to her knees with disappointment, but the only thing she could do right that moment was respond to his muffled protests on the other side. "Charlotte. Charlotte. Come on. Don't be like this."

She searched for her voice and mustered all the

nerve she had left. "Just to make it clear, I said nothing is changing on this end. Except whether or not I'll ever let you back."

CHAPTER NINE

JACKSON WASN'T EVEN sure how he'd made the drive home. His head swam with thoughts yet nothing seemed clear enough to grasp. Charlotte was pregnant, the one thing they'd both agreed from the start would never happen.

And she planned to keep the baby.

Where did that leave him? With an intense sense of déjà vu.

Think straight!

First, he needed to admit he loved her for helping him get his life back, and though he'd been on the verge of telling her—his midnight visit had seemed like the perfect time—the news that she was pregnant had knocked him completely off track. It had rocked the thoughts in his brain until they were so jumbled up he couldn't think.

The monumental revelation, that he loved something Charlotte had done for him, helping him heal and grow, deserved its own moment in time. He'd planned to indulge in the new thought for days to come, that he might be able to love again, to hold the concept in his hands and pass it back and forth, to get a feel for it, savoring the secret, and then and only then to find the nerve to say it out loud. To see how it sounded: *Charlotte, you've revived me, and I'm finally open to a complete relationship with you. Are you ready to see where this goes?*

It might sound awkward and clinical, but it was his true feeling, and she deserved to know.

But she'd just told him she was pregnant!

Now he'd have to jump ahead dozens of steps in the relationship to admit the big secret. The one he'd planned to carry around with him for days, taking his own sweet time to tease her with dumb grins, special touches, secret glances at work, all building to the big revelation. *I'm in love with you, can't you tell?* Now everything had changed. Because the pregnancy forced it. And long before he was ready he had to admit it. The truth shocked him, made his mouth go dry. This was never supposed to happen again.

She wasn't merely "a thing." She hadn't ever been. He loved her. Damn it, he loved her. But there wasn't time or the luxury of basking in that knowledge because she was already making him a father. Again.

Part of him wanted to kick himself for getting into this position in the first place. Wasn't a man supposed to learn from his history? Why had he let himself think he could be normal, pick up his life, enjoy getting close with a woman again? He'd been playing with fire since he'd first asked her out. If only Charlotte hadn't made it so enticing and easy.

Sure, blame her. You wanted her long before she came around to the idea. His fingers flew to his brows and rubbed up and down, as if that might help clear his head.

He'd sat there just now at her house like a big dolt when she'd told him. His jaw had dropped open, mind numbed by the news, unable to respond. *This is all out of order. I need more time to get used to the first part! You're not just a thing to me. I think I love you.*

He'd seen her inconsolable reaction, as clear

as her beautiful brown eyes. He'd hurt her to the marrow, ripped open her heart, left her bleeding, and she'd turned that hurt into anger and kicked him out. Could he blame her?

He paced his condo, unable to rest, wanting to call her but still not knowing what to say. *I love you but I'm not ready for more.*

A baby? He was forty-two, done with those things. They'd made a pact on their first date, hadn't they? She clearly hadn't keep her side of the bargain. But was that all they were to each other, a bargain? He stopped to breathe and felt the wall building itself around him, separating him from the living, keeping him safe from ever feeling again.

Was he done with Charlotte? Could he throw away that new love so easily? What kind of man walked away from a woman he'd finally and only just recently admitted he loved, because she was pregnant and he didn't want to be a father again?

An empty and damaged-for-life bastard, that was who. Write it down, put it in his packet— damaged goods. But was that who he really was?

Now was the time to decide if he was still that other man. Or not.

He slid onto his couch, mind roiling, hands fisted, sweat beading on his upper lip. He wanted a stiff drink, the crutch he'd come to rely on years before. But he'd spent enough time on the dark side after the accident. He knew the path to hell backward and forward and never wanted to go there again. He'd traded in that prison cell for a new beginning in California. Which had opened him up...for Charlotte.

He called her. She didn't answer. He didn't leave a message.

He glanced at his watch—it was almost three a.m. His first surgery was scheduled for seven. He put on a pot of coffee, set the brew button for five a.m. then went to his bedroom, threw on his jogging shorts and exchanged his prosthetic for the running blade, then drove to Malibu for a long soul-searching run on the beach just before dawn. Maybe it would help clear his head.

Having a full surgical schedule would force him to compartmentalize. Charlotte deserved his undivided attention and so did his patients. He could only deal with one trauma at a time, and one hundred percent couldn't be divided during surgery. As much as it tore him up, since she hadn't answered earlier, he'd have to wait until that night to talk to Charlotte. Maybe he'd be more coherent by then.

In the meantime he worried what kind of a hard-hearted SOB she'd think he was. Because he cared. And because he was leaving her in limbo for a day, he deserved all of her negative thoughts about him. He could practically feel them with each step of his run. His pace was off, his muscles tight and tender, his breathing out of sync. Yeah, he deserved it for putting her through hell.

The problem with taking the "patients come first" approach in medicine was that when at the end of an unbelievably grueling day, when he hadn't had an hour's sleep the night before and had zero left to give, he wound up giving himself a pass on calling Charlotte. *I need to be well rested, to have my thoughts straight, to know exactly what I think and feel about the situation*, he rationalized. He hadn't had a moment to think about any of it that day, and with tomorrow's schedule he feared it would be no different then.

She'd probably be done with him by then. And he would deserve it. So he dialed her number again. She didn't pick up. Again.

He fell into bed, planning to call her once more in an hour, and amazingly slept through the night instead. But at five a.m. he was wide-awake, his head spinning with thoughts. It was too early to call her, so he dressed for another run. He needed to consider the consequences of his affair with the beautiful pathologist. The woman he loved. He was starting to get used to the phrase, the woman he loved. That was progress, wasn't it? Maybe by the time he had finished jogging, she'd be up. He'd call her. This time she might answer.

But what would he say? Could he make things right with her after this torturing delay?

It wasn't a good run—in fact, it was worse than the day before. Every step felt as sluggish as his brain. Anxious thoughts came to mind. How much he missed Charlotte. How he needed to talk to her, which left him edgy and stepping up his pace. One he could hardly keep up with.

After the unheroic way he'd handled her news, why would she even want anything to do with him? She'd pushed him out of her house. Her life? Hell, maybe it was better to let things end as they had.

He wanted to kick himself for letting the negative and completely unacceptable thought slip in.

It was an old and sorry excuse, as familiar as a predictable movie. And totally unacceptable. Wasn't he a new man—a healing man, thanks to Charlotte—or had her news ripped off the new skin and left him back where he'd started three years ago with all of his old flaws alive and festering, dragging him down?

Was that really what he was made of? He hated to think of the answer. He was only forty-two, it had been over three years since everything had changed, and surely he was a better man now.

He stopped and called her. As predicted, it went directly to message. "Charlotte, we need to talk. When can I see you?"

He ran on, soon hearing a text message shoot through. Don't bother to call again.

Blast it all to hell. He really had blown it by letting the extra day go by!

Damn, he already missed her more than he had ever thought possible. His chest ached, fearing he'd lost her forever. She was pregnant with his baby. Their baby. He understood what an epic decision it had to be for her to have the baby. Her fears, her guilt of passing on imperfect genes. He wanted to be by her side every step of the way. Now all he had to do was convince her he wasn't the heel she must think he was.

Not an easy task.

He ran back to his car, remembering how important the role of being a father was, and how his wife had always complained he had never been there enough for the boys. If he was a new man, couldn't he be the kind of father for this baby that he hadn't been for his sons? Charlotte was giving him a chance to shine in life again. Together. Why would he want to crawl back to his "you call this living" cocoon?

Things could be completely different this time if she'd only give him a chance. Shouldn't she give him a break? Sure, he'd failed his first chance, when she'd told him the news. He could tell how hard her decision must have been—she'd looked like she'd been through the wringer. The fine skin beneath those beautiful eyes had looked bruised and tense. Her full, normally soft mouth bitten and tight. She'd left work early and had probably thought about her condition every second until she'd called him. She'd cautiously tiptoed her feelings out, testing him, and had blown him away with her words. "I'm crazy about you."

She'd put herself on the line and he could have been a robot for the lack of response he'd given her. Of course she'd be furious with him. In his defense, he'd been completely stunned. But he'd had time to recover, and all he'd chosen to do had been to let her down in the name of needing time to think things through and his demanding job. No wonder she never wanted to hear from him again.

He got into his car, wondering what good was a man who didn't risk it all for the woman he loved? Yeah, he'd had enough time to admit it and now he knew without a doubt that he *loved* her. Maybe he'd been forced to come to the conclusion, but the feeling had already been there, well hidden, of course, because even a breath of admitting he could love again had scared the hell out of him, let alone the thought of becoming a dad again. He knew he wouldn't feel the love so strongly now if it hadn't already been there, starting as a seed and growing every time they'd seen each other. Why else had everything felt so right whenever they'd been together?

He drove to her town house and pushed the security button.

"Go away." Her voice came through the speaker a few seconds later.

"I need to talk to you."

She clicked off and didn't open the gate for him. After a few minutes he revised his plan. Because now that he'd had an epiphany, he knew what needed to be done. If life was all about what was happening right then, not the past or what might be in the future, he wanted and needed with everything he had to be there for Charlotte *now*. And when the time came, he'd be a proper father for their kid, too. That was the beauty of new beginnings—he could start afresh, get it right this time.

He glanced at his watch. It was almost six on Thursday morning and he had another big surgery in less than two hours. Tomorrow, Friday, was the day they were supposed to leave for Georgia and his cousin's wedding. He'd bought the plane tickets and made reservations at the grand old hotel on the banks of the Savannah River. But forget about the wedding. He wouldn't go unless Charlotte was by his side. There was no way he'd go without her.

He'd been told all his life he was smart, but what this situation called for wasn't brains. It called for heart...plus a bit of resourcefulness. For a methodical surgeon, every once in a while he surprised himself with his creativity. A great idea popped into his mind. Sure, it was a risk, a huge risk, which made it all the more necessary. Charlotte had done the same with him the night before last, had laid it all out there. Now it was his turn. She deserved no less. The only question was, how would Charlotte respond to his over-the-top plan?

* * *

It was seven a.m. Jackson had performed the five-minute hand and arm scrub, and donned the first pair of his sterile double gloves. His surgical nurse had just helped him into his gown, his cap and mask were in place, and he used his elbow to push the plate on the automatic door opener on the wall. The important surgery required a frozen section. He'd seen Dr. Gordon's name on the list for the morning, so he'd called and, calling in a favor, had insisted that Dr. Johnson had to do it. It would be up to Jim Gordon, now that he was back part-time at work, to come up with a believable reason for Charlotte to step in. Knowing what a team player Jim was, Jackson trusted it would be a good one, too.

An hour later, after they'd cracked open the patient's chest and he'd biopsied the mass on the right lung, he put the fresh tissue into the waiting petri dish, which was sealed and labeled and quickly handed over to the OR runner. Pathology knew the specimen was coming. "Don't give it to anyone but Dr. Johnson."

"Yes, sir." The young summer volunteer, garbed

in full OR regalia, took the specimen and fled like his life depended on the mission. Did he even know who Dr. Johnson was?

The entire surgical team waited for the report as the surgery was held in limbo and the patient constantly monitored.

While he waited, leaving the assistant surgeon in charge, he knew beyond a doubt what he had to do once he heard Charlotte's voice. He wanted to be a man Charlotte could trust and depend on and look to for support, for everything, and he didn't intend to waste another minute before he told her.

Within five minutes he heard Charlotte's voice on the OR intercom. There was a noticeably cool clip to it. "The lung biopsy is benign for cancer."

Great news for the patient, though it was imperative for pathology to figure out exactly what the mass was with further studies. He cleared his throat before Charlotte could disconnect. He couldn't let it matter that he'd be in front of the entire surgical team and anyone who was within earshot in the pathology department. This was too important, and now was the time for desperate measures.

"Charlotte?"

A second, then two passed. "Yes?"

"This is Jackson, just to make it clear."

Another pause. "Yes."

He took a deep breath. "I never thought I'd have a shotgun wedding at forty-two, and I can't exactly get on bended knee here in surgery." The staff laughed and looked surprised, but when they realized he wasn't kidding around, everyone stopped to listen to what in the world he would say next. "But, Charlotte, will you marry me?"

"P-pardon me?" she stammered. "We're on the speakerphone, Jackson."

"I know. And I don't care. You won't take my calls and I figured if I came down there you wouldn't see me. So, with the OR staff as my witnesses, I'm asking, will you marry me?" Then, taking the biggest risk of his life, well, after proposing in front of almost a dozen people, he said, "I'll give you some time to think." Then he nodded for his surgical nurse to click off the intercom.

The instant she did, the operating-room team broke into applause.

He tried to ignore them, having a patient lying on the OR table and all, though he felt fantastic, like he'd just climbed Mount Everest, and smiled beneath his mask. He'd done it. Excellent. A wave of insecurity knocked him back a bit. His stunt didn't guarantee a "yes" from Charlotte, but at least he'd made his case loud and clear. With witnesses! He loved her. He wanted to marry her.

Now forcing his personal life to the back of his brain, he focused on the patient, who deserved to be front and center. When he'd finished resecting the rest of the mass and tying off all involved vessels, he asked the assistant surgeon to close for him. He knew and trusted the young woman's skill. Plus the team was completely on board with him needing to leave.

He disposed of his dirty gowns and gloves, washed his hands again, then strode to the doctors' lockers. He grabbed his work kit and headed to the bathroom to clean up and shave, to make himself as presentable as he could possibly be, before facing the woman he loved. Once he passed the mirror test, he gave himself a reassuring nod. "You've got this."

First off, he stopped to speak to the family of his lung surgery patient, sharing his good report, watching the tension vanish from their eyes and foreheads. Then, on his way to the elevator, while passing through the surgical ward, he noticed a patient getting discharged and there was a beautiful bouquet remaining at the bedside on the movable table. The staff rolled the table out of the room and into the hall in order to get the patient into the wheelchair in the tiny private room.

"You taking this?" he asked.

"No. I don't want to be reminded of this place," the young man said. "Flowers aren't my thing anyway."

"Mind if I borrow them?"

"Take 'em, they're yours."

Jackson removed the bright white daisies and yellow sunflowers from the glass vase and shook off the excess water. He grabbed some paper towels from the nearby dispenser to wrap around the stems. Pleased it was a proper enough bouquet, one fit for following up on a marriage proposal, he headed down to the basement and the pathology department. Since he didn't have a ring to offer her, these bright summer flowers would have to do.

Charlotte stood bewildered, staring at the OR intercom in the tiny room with the cryostat machine. Jackson had just asked her to marry him. The thought set off full body chills. The good kind. This after she'd spent the last two days trying to force him out of her life and heart. And had failed miserably. Was he serious? He wouldn't dare play a cruel joke on her, would he?

Of course not!

She'd laid a huge surprise on him the other night, then had gone ballistic when he'd been as stunned as she was right now. He'd needed time to think through the sudden life change rather than jump up and down with joy. Hell, *she* hadn't felt joyful when she'd got the news, yet she'd expected him to be. How unfair and unrealistic she'd been. But being frightened about her decision to become a mother, a decision as momentous as her double mastectomy surgery, she'd needed his instant support. Unreasonably so. And he'd been unable to give it to her right off. So she'd got mad.

It'd hurt, and sent her back to feeling like a needy teenager when her father had offered little support over the death of her mother. She'd freaked out and pushed Jackson out the door. Out of her life? She didn't know for sure because she couldn't think clearly at the time. All she knew was he hadn't met her unrealistic and unreasonable needs, so he'd become a villain.

Two miserable days later, deep down she knew without a doubt he was anything but.

He'd pleaded with her to understand, to give him time to think, to let him back in. Yet she'd said something hurtful and angry through the door about whether or not she'd ever let him back. How immature.

It hadn't been fair to him, not by a long shot. Most guys would have just walked away and given up. *Her loss*, they could have rationalized. Yet Jackson had just pulled the craziest stunt she could ever imagine. He'd proposed over an OR intercom, with his entire surgical staff listening in. That proved he loved her, didn't it?

She smiled, tears welled in her eyes and she pushed them away. Except he had yet to say the words.

Now it was perfectly clear why Dr. Gordon had made that shabby excuse for not being able to do his scheduled assignment for the morning. She'd checked the surgery lineup and had seen Jackson's name and nearly lost her breakfast. They'd conspired against her.

Someone cleared their throat. She turned to see her mentor, who'd stepped around from being just on the other side of the laboratory wall. Though thinner than he used to be, the flash was back in his old eyes. "That was quite a scene," he said, unable to hide his pleasure.

"Did you know he was going to do that?"

"To propose? No. But he begged me to make you do the frozen section. What was a man to do?"

She shook her head, letting herself float on air just a little. What a stunt, asking a woman to marry him with an audience. Yet *not* hearing the most important part first, *I love you*, kept her tethered to the ground. He was going the traditional, honorable route. Girl gets pregnant, the guy marries her. It was probably a golden rule of the South. Was she supposed to clap her hands in joy? Was this what she truly wanted?

Dr. Gordon stepped closer and patted her back. Her mixed-up tears kept coming. It was great to have him at work again, even if only part-time, and for how long, no one could possibly guess. She was especially glad he'd been in on the most amazing proposal she could ever have dreamed of—minus a single phrase.

"I hope you have the good sense to tell him yes."

She went quiet, in all honesty not knowing for sure what her answer would be. "I'll let you know when I figure it out."

With that, they walked back to their respective offices, where piles of patient slides awaited their diagnoses.

She took her seat in front of the microscope, adjusting the head, resting her nose between the eyepieces, and, still feeling as light as a feather with hope and love, she focused on the slide in the tray holder. From time to time, though, she considered how she'd forced Jackson into the corner, and being the wonderful man he was, he couldn't stand to let her down. She worried she'd never know for sure if he loved her or was only doing his Southern gentleman duty. The honorable thing.

Would that be good enough?

Charlotte spent the next hour and a half in her darkened office with the shine of his big moment and proposal fading, reading slides, trying to put the man she loved out of her mind. A nearly impossible task. What would she tell him?

Her door flew open, the light was turned on, and in barged Jackson. She jumped. "I believe we left off at the part where I asked you to marry me." He pushed the flowers at her.

Enough time had passed for her to come off her cloud—in fact, with her growing doubt those clouds had turned a pale shade of gray. She didn't want to force him into doing something he didn't truly want. With a guarded heart she spoke. "You don't have to do me any favors, Jackson." She took the flowers anyway, laid them on her desk. He looked puzzled, as if he couldn't believe that she still didn't get it.

Jackson had been so swept away with carrying out his risky task, he'd forgotten some very important words. He'd managed to mangle the proposal. What a mess. The whole thing had started with Charlotte feeling insecure about being pregnant and having to break the news to him, a guy who'd never wanted to get married or have kids again. He needed her to know something.

"Forgive me. I forgot to tell you something first—the most important part." Jackson approached Charlotte's chair and took her hands, bringing her to standing so he could look into those warm brown, though suddenly skeptical, eyes. He noticed her hands were shaking, and for a guy who'd just performed flawless surgery, his hands were, too. Why wouldn't they be? They were both about to embark on the biggest journey of their lives. This time together. If he could get Charlotte to cooperate, that was.

"I want to be there for our baby, Charlotte."

"And?"

"And? Oh, of course, and you! I want to be there for you."

"Because?" Now she looked downright impatient.

Because? Oh, for crying out loud, he really was sleep deprived and not thinking straight. "I love you. Didn't I say it?" In all honesty, the proposal in the OR, fueled by anxiety and adrenaline, was a blur.

"No."

Damn. He'd blown it big-time, but couldn't she read between the lines? "But I asked you to marry me. Surely that implies that? You know—"

She canted her head as if he'd been singing a beautiful aria and had just hit a sour note. He could fix that.

"I love you." He hoped the sincerity he felt down to his bones was reflected in his eyes, because he needed her to understand how important this was to him. "I want to marry you, to be our baby's father, if you'll have me." She gazed at him, not as much as a whisper crossing her lips. He needed to step up his pitch. Maybe appeal to her practical side? "You'll need my help raising our kid because you have no clue what you're getting yourself into. Trust me, you need me. Our kid needs me." He would have missed her twitch of a smile if he'd blinked, because he was sweating through what had turned out to be a totally messed-up proposal. He hoped she needed him half as much as he needed her, now that he'd finally admitted it. He let go of her hands and framed her face then kissed her with everything he had, trying to communicate what he couldn't somehow manage to find the perfect words for. She kissed him back. A good sign. It occurred that she might need to hear him say it again. "I need you, because I love you. Marry me. Please."

She fell against him, and he held her tight.

"We've had a rocky patch," she said to his chest before she looked up at him. "It took a couple of days for you to come to your decision."

"You mean my senses."

"Yes." She smiled, but not joyfully, more of a sad or resigned kind of smile. Could his delay in figuring things out have taken that much life out of her? "Like you, I'd like to take some time to think over your proposal."

Had his hesitation and two days' lag time been enough to make her question what they had? He had no right to demand an answer right now, not after what he'd done, but it hurt to the center of his heart, realizing how he'd left her alone when she'd needed him most. Now he could say he truly knew how she'd felt. All he could do was hope she'd come to her senses the way he had and say yes. Yes to their future. "I don't want to wait that long, but I have to understand after what I've put you through."

"It isn't payback, Jackson. I've got to think things over."

Suddenly feeling like a man walking a tight-rope, he went still. "That's understandable." What would he do if she told him no? He didn't want to let her out of his sight but he had to finish his afternoon clinic and tie things up for the next few days away. "What about the wedding this weekend? Will you still go to Savannah with me?"

She kissed him lightly, then looked into his eyes. "Yes. I promised I'd go with you and I'll go."

That gave him time and the chance to make things right again. If he couldn't convince her that he loved her right now, maybe the beauty of his hometown would help her fall in love.

CHAPTER TEN

LATE ON FRIDAY night Charlotte stood at the window of her tenth-story hotel room in Savannah, watching a foreign container ship slowly pass by. The tall rusted ship loaded several stories high with colorful cargo crates almost reached her eye level. Definitely a working ship. With tons and tons of cargo, how could it possibly stay afloat?

"That thing's huge," she said loudly to Jackson, who was arranging clothes in the closet.

"Get used to it—this is one of the most traveled rivers for international shipping in the US."

"It's really fascinating. I kind of feel like the captain could be watching me with his binoculars."

"I wouldn't be surprised. Probably hoping to get a peep show."

That made her laugh. "Boy, would he be disappointed."

Out of nowhere Jackson was at her back, passing his arms around her waist and pulling her close and nuzzling her neck. "He wouldn't get the chance because I'd deck him if he tried spying on you."

She turned her head so they could kiss. "Thanks." She looked back at the ship, almost directly across from them. "Did you see that, Captain?" she called out.

Jackson chuckled along with her and hugged her closer.

It was the first time they'd gone away overnight and checked into a hotel room together, and the first time they'd cuddled today. He'd chosen a gorgeous and grand hotel and spa with a harbor view. Every detail about the place spoke of old wealth. For a San Fernando Valley girl who'd grown up in a lower middle class area, the obvious opulence, though beautiful and inviting, also made her a little uncomfortable. Even now, she'd never think to stay in such a place, but apparently the man with three names and a number was in his element.

Their spacious bedroom had plenty of room

246 WEDDING DATE WITH THE ARMY DOC

to sit on the love seat and enjoy the view. Like a grand lady wearing a shiny pearl necklace, the Savannah River looked extra pretty with the city lights from across the river.

"What's all that?" She pointed across the river to a long street still busy with activity at the late hour. Rather than deal with what was written on her heart, for now she'd stick to superficial talk. Which was pretty much what they'd done for the entire flight to Georgia.

"That's River Street. All those buildings used to be cotton warehouses. Now they've been converted into anything your heart desires."

"Wow."

She looked downward at the huge hotel pool accented with lights, then to the right where a white gazebo adorned in tiny café lights looked like a miniature toy in the center of a picture-perfect lawn. All the while, as she checked out the area, she enjoyed the warmth of Jackson's body against hers, his hands resting on her stomach. It made her think of their baby and how protected it was right this moment. "Looks like they have weddings here, too."

"They have weddings everywhere in Savannah. It's a very romantic city. I can't wait to show you the historic district tomorrow morning."

"In that case, I hate to be a party pooper, but since we've got a big day tomorrow I'd better get some sleep. I'm worn out from the flight and getting up so early." *And being pregnant and totally confused about your marriage proposal.* She glanced at her watch and realized that back home it was only eight o'clock. Was that what pregnancy did to a woman?

"I wanted to introduce you to an old college buddy of mine—we were roommates—but I can understand your needing more rest these days." Jackson had been completely accommodating the entire day, and now was no different. "You've got to take care of our baby, right?"

That was part of the problem. Since Jackson had come around and said he wanted to marry her and he loved her, she couldn't quite shake the feeling it was all about the baby. "I had no idea how exhausting being pregnant was."

He squeezed her a little tighter. "And I don't want to make you feel worse by pushing too hard.

The point is for you to enjoy the wedding tomorrow evening. To enjoy Savannah." He kissed her cheek. "Would you mind if I met up with Jarod for drinks downstairs in the bar?"

"Of course not. Go right ahead."

"Okay, I won't be late. Just a drink and a little catching up on things."

Within ten minutes of Jackson leaving, Charlotte had done her nighttime routine and snuggled into the amazingly comfortable bed, choosing to leave the curtains open so she could continue to look outside before going to sleep. She may not have the energy to be out there, but she could still enjoy the hustle and bustle of River Street across the river. She was also rewarded with the grand entrance of another enormous cargo ship passing slowly through the waters. The sight put a smile on her face, making her feel oddly connected with the wide world while snug in her bed.

Unfortunately, she couldn't shut down her mind or stop her worries about Jackson. Honor was a large part of who he was, and she worried he was merely doing the right thing by asking her to marry him because she'd got pregnant. Just like he'd done with his ex-wife. Before the weekend was over she'd have to confront him about it. With her body dictating her needs, plus the fact she'd hardly slept last night from thinking nonstop about Jackson's true motives for proposing, within a few minutes she'd drifted off to sleep.

She heard voices and forced her eyes open. Glancing next to her in the bed, there was evidence that Jackson had slept there, and she remembered cuddling next to him at one point in the night, but he wasn't there now. Plus the sheets felt cold. How long had he been up? And who was he talking to? Should she hide under the blankets and play possum?

"Thank you," Jackson said, then closed the hotel-room door, before shortly appearing at her bedside with a full breakfast tray.

She sat up, mouth open. "Wow."

"Good morning, sunshine! Breakfast is served."

She had to hand it to him, he was really trying hard—the least she could do was be gracious.

She glanced at the digital clock on the bedside table. It was only seven-thirty in the morning.

That would be four-thirty back home. "I feel like a princess. Thank you." She hoped the current wave of morning queasiness would pass so she could really enjoy the spread, rather than move things around her plate and hope he didn't notice. Especially after his obvious desire to treat her like royalty. She sipped some water. "Did you sleep much last night?" She threw back the covers, and in her sexy nightgown, which hung a little loosely around her chest, she stood.

Jackson came to her and hugged her good morning. They lingered in their embrace and she savored his solid warmth and the way he smelled fresh from the shower complete with yet a new aftershave, this one with a hint of sandalwood. Dared she dream about being his wife, secure in knowing it was her he wanted to marry, and not merely because of a ready-made family?

"Yeah, I was in before one. Had a good talk with my buddy. Got all caught up on a few things." It made her wonder if he'd talked about his current situation, having a pregnant girlfriend and having to get married *again*, but she didn't ask. It was too early for drama. "Let's eat. We've got a big day ahead of us."

"I'll do my best," she said, smiling up at him, hoping she'd make it through the day with such a heavy heart.

"There are twenty-two squares to share with you."

She popped her eyes wide open. "Twenty-two?"

"I drive fast, but we'll only have time for a few today, my favorites like Lafayette Square, Chippewa Square, Monterey Square and I'll tell you all about the Mercer house then. Oh, then we'll stop by Ellis Square so we can hit City Market. I've got a favorite restaurant there where we can have lunch. Then tomorrow we can spend a little more time checking out more squares. How's that sound?"

It sounded wonderful, but it surprised her that he hadn't marked out time for his family or for introducing her. Could he feel ashamed of the fact that, if she said yes, he'd be having another "shotgun wedding," as he'd called it in the OR? But she didn't want to spoil his enthusiasm first thing in the morning, so she kept her uncomfortable thoughts to herself.

"Great!" She glanced at the tray of breakfast food and thought about the wedding that evening. "But that sounds like a lot of eating."

He laughed. "Can you tell I'm really excited to have you here?" He sat and slathered a piece of toast with Georgia peach jam.

Maybe she should try to believe him. He wanted to share his world with her, and that knowledge set off a warm feeling tumbling through her body. Her queasiness vanished and she was suddenly more than ready to dive into the scrambled eggs and O'Brien potatoes. And, mmm, the fresh fruit and pancakes looked good, too!

Charlotte had never seen such a picturesque area as the historic district in Savannah. While they drove, she felt like she'd gone back in time with the beautifully preserved buildings and famous blocked-off squares, each with its own charm and individual appeal. Spanish moss draped every tree, and there were hundreds of oak trees throughout the area, as well as palmettos and magnolias.

"Lucky for you you're here in summer to see the crepe myrtles bloom."

The heat made her feel sticky, and she wasn't convinced she should feel lucky to be here in the heart of summer, but she completely agreed that the crepe myrtles were gorgeous. She was also glad he'd put on the air conditioner for the drive. "They certainly are beautiful. But with all the trees everywhere, everything looks beautiful here."

Jackson lucked out and found a parking spot. "We've actually got a nickname as the forest city because of that." He helped her out of the car and a wave of hot humidity hit her like a wet sauna towel. "But with heat like this, our ancestors had to plant trees just for the shade to survive. It was a practical idea that's brought all kinds of benefits."

She fanned herself as she felt a fine sheen of perspiration cover her face, wondering how crazy it would make her hair. Yeah, lucky her for being in Georgia in August. As a San Fernando Valley girl, she certainly knew about heat, but the humidity here brought "hot" to a new level. As they walked, she wondered how the bride would survive wearing a wedding dress in weather like this. She knew the wedding was out toward the beach at a lighthouse, which would probably help.

Holding hands and strolling to the heart of Ellis Square, they watched the children and a few adults playing in the big fountain, which was obviously meant for water play. The sight of little kids squealing with joy as the dancing water shot up made her think of her baby. She looked at the man she'd been positive she loved a few short days ago.

He pointed to the busy market and shop area. "Ever had shrimp and grits?"

"Had shrimp. Never grits."

"I'm going to take you for the gourmet supreme version of that dish. Follow me."

During lunch, she ventured to bring up one major portion of her worries. "Jackson, what if this baby is a girl?"

"Is that what's been on your mind?"

She nodded. "In part. Yes."

"You've got to quit thinking of yourself as poison for a girl baby."

"But if I pass on my genes…"

"You can't let yourself obsess about that. We could have a boy. Or a girl who'll be perfectly fine. If you want to have her tested, I'll stand behind you, but worrying and feeling guilty isn't going to help anything. Who knows where breast cancer research will be in twenty years? Please, stop doubting yourself. Think about the wonder of having a baby. Period. Not a single child born is guaranteed to come problem free."

Moved by his sentiment, she reached across the table and touched his arm. This was part of what she loved about him. "Are you really okay with me being pregnant?"

"Once I got used to the idea, I have to say I'm excited. It'll give me a chance to be the kind of father I should have been with my sons. I promise to be there for you, to help you raise our kid."

She believed him and burst into tears to prove it, but what he'd just vowed had sounded more like a dutiful co-parent than a loving husband. If she could only believe he felt as strongly for her.

After a huge lunch, and visiting a couple more beautifully impressive town squares, Jackson was considerate about Charlotte needing to rest before they got ready for the wedding. So he delivered her back to the hotel room so she could take a power nap and he headed out to the gym and then the pool. She definitely wanted to look her best for the wedding that night, for meeting his family, too, but most especially for him. She needed to see the love in his eyes before she made up her mind about his marriage proposal.

"Wow!" was all that came out of Jackson's mouth. Charlotte stood before him in a pale peach-colored dress that flowed in tiers to her ankles with a snug and wide fitted waist and a halter-style top embellished with a beaded and jeweled collar.

"The color is called blush." She looked anxiously down at her dress toward her toes. "I chose it because it works with my complexion. Plus I thought it would be complementary no matter what the bride's colors are."

As far as he was concerned, she didn't need to explain anything. Indeed, her light olive skin and dark hair glowed in contrast to the pastel shade. "You were meant for that dress, or I should probably say that dress was meant for you."

She smiled shyly and turned a slow circle, causing the skirt to flare out the slightest bit. The cut of the back of the dress was high, she hadn't gone for sexy other than a slit opening beneath the halter collar, yet she still looked like the sexiest woman on the earth to him.

"Thank you. Too bad I'll only get to wear it once."

The ironic statement made him grin. Not if his plans played out as expected. "After the bride, you'll be the most beautiful woman there." Because heaven help any woman who tried to show up the bride!

She shook her head, like she couldn't believe him. Anyone seeing her would never have a clue she'd had bilateral mastectomies. He hoped that didn't still make her feel self-conscious. How many times had he proved she was all he ever wanted or needed? He saw her as the woman he loved, a completely beautiful person, sexy and appealing, and though she had scars, they were part of her. Part of who he loved and wanted to spend the rest of his life with. Like the missing part of his leg was part of who he was now. The guy he'd finally accepted, with the help of Charlotte.

"Those sandals are a knockout, too." She wore strappy beaded silver sandals and had had a flashy pedicure. Though he'd memorized her body with all the times they'd made love, he'd never realized how sexy her feet were. Wow. "I may have to get a special permit to take you out in public. You might cause accidents and general chaos."

She smiled demurely and blushed, and he took a mental picture of that perfect moment in time to cherish and keep in his heart forever. Until she said yes to his marriage proposal, he couldn't let down his guard. He really wanted this. A life with her. Without a doubt. Now he had to convince her.

It wasn't until they got into his rented car that a tight coil started knotting in his stomach. He was ready to see his parents, had talked extensively to them about his plans for this trip back home. That wasn't the problem. He and Evan had worked things out, but Andrew was still avoiding him, and that hurt. Otherwise, if Andrew had been open to it, he would have spent time with him earlier today. The one break he'd caught had been Evaline deciding not to attend the wedding. That had taken a huge weight off his mind.

From what he'd heard, talking to his parents, well, mostly from his mother, Kiefer's future wife, Ashley, was a councilwoman from the tough town of Southriver and the wedding would be attended by the locals and act as a big thanks to her for helping revitalize her home front. She and his cousin Kiefer had met when he'd become the director of the new neighborhood clinic. People would be attending from all walks of life from blue collar up to high society. It should be an interesting mix. Knowing his community activist aunt Maggie, she was probably thrilled by Kiefer's choice of a wife. Since he and Kiefer had always kept in touch, especially as they were both doctors, Jackson knew he'd be welcomed.

Due to summer traffic it took Jackson almost twice as long as it normally should to reach Tybee

Island Lighthouse Station. But what perfect timing for Mother Nature, at just about sunset. Once they'd parked, they headed toward a huge white tent set up on rich green grass next to the famous lighthouse, black with one wide white stripe in the center. It sat in the middle of five historic support buildings, a perfect little community. It had been made into a museum compound in 1961 and people lined up to have their weddings here. In the backdrop the sun quickly made plans to set in the west. To the east, the Atlantic Ocean made itself known with a light breeze scented with salty sea air. It lifted Charlotte's hair, which looked fuller and wavier since they'd got out of the car.

What could he say but she was the most beautiful woman in the world. His peaceful, loving observation quickly got jostled by his mother's strident voice.

"Jackson, yoo-hoo!"

He turned. "Hi, Mom." Her hair may be going silver and white, but there was no mistaking his mother's sharp blue eyes hadn't lost a hint of their passion for life.

She grabbed him and hugged him as if he were

still a kid. "Look at you—you look so hand-some!" He fought a grimace. "And this must be Charlotte. Aren't you lovely. Hi, I'm Georgina, Jackie's mom."

She greeted Charlotte in the same exuberant way, making her almost lose her balance. "It's great to meet you."

"You'll have to sit at our table later so we can get to know each other, okay?"

"That'd be great."

Did they have a choice? But Charlotte was being a wonderful sport, and he loved her even more for it. Off in the distance he noticed Evan, who waved to him, then shortly brought Andrew over. The fact that Drew smiled, and it seemed sincere, when they said hello meant the world to Jackson. Maybe all was not lost between him and his elder son, and maybe mending his relation-ship with Evan had helped. He'd make a point to talk to Andrew tonight, and to invite him out for a visit to California. Fingers crossed Drew would be open to that.

Music started to play as the sunset was im-minent, and the open seating quickly filled up.

Jackson guided Charlotte to the closest available seats. By the look of the large crowd, Ashley and Kiefer had a lot of friends in their community.

Handsome as always, tall, with brown hair and having Aunt Maggie's green eyes, Kiefer stood with the lighthouse as a backdrop in a dark suit, waiting for his bride. Ashley soon appeared in a classic white dress but with a light green sash, dark shoulder-length hair and eyes that reminded him of Charlotte's. She looked pretty and proud. She held her head high and smiled with all her heart at her friends and family as she walked down the aisle, but most of all she smiled for his cousin.

Jackson felt it in his gut—these two were meant for each other. Then he glanced at Charlotte, eyes bright with excitement over the wedding, the setting, the couple, and that same gut reaction helped him know he'd made the right decision in asking her to marry him. Now, if she'd only realize they were meant for each other and say yes.

The reception was a bit chaotic, thanks to the standing-room-only crowd and the low-key wedding plans, but everyone still managed to get fed.

A local group played typical wedding reception songs, and Jackson even convinced Charlotte to dance with him a few times. He'd never get tired of the feel of her in his arms.

He didn't want to push the point, but she hadn't given him an answer yet. He was kind of hoping she'd get all swept away with the wedding tonight and tell him yes. The music was romantic, they were dancing, and it was time to prod things along. "You know I love you, right?"

Hope showed in her gaze. She rested her forehead on his cheek. "I know I love *you*."

He squeezed her tighter. "So let's get married." The song ended. No answer. He didn't want to let go of her, so he stood holding her close until the makeshift dance floor had cleared. She took a breath. He waited for her to say something.

"When are you going to come visit me?" the familiar voice of his grandfather called out from the edge of the dance floor.

Jackson led Charlotte to where he sat. "Gramps, this is Charlotte Johnson."

"Miss Johnson, it's my pleasure to meet you." His wiry, silver-eyed and white-haired granddaddy looked enchanted, and had obviously partaken of the champagne punch. She sat beside him and let him continue to hold her hand. They chatted briefly about the weather, where she'd grown up and a few other superficial topics. Then Gramps jumped right to the heart of things. "I've been around over eighty years, and I think I can judge when a man is smitten with a woman. It seems Jackson the Third here is sportin' the look of a man in love. So I must ask you, are you the one who put it there?"

Her hand flew to her chest as her cheeks blushed. Jackson could tell she didn't know whether to take his granddad seriously or not.

"I don't want to speak for Charlotte, Gramps, but I can answer that question easy enough. Yes."

Her gaze flashed to his and he didn't waver. If there was ever a time for her to know how he felt, it was now. Any man willing to get called out by his grandfather for being in love deserved an answer to his proposal. But he sensed she still wasn't ready, and he didn't want to force the point, so he let the moment pass.

"There you are!" Kiefer said. "I finally tracked you down."

Jackson greeted his cousin and made the proper introductions between the bride and groom and Charlotte. He almost spewed his champagne when out of the blue Ashley asked if another wedding was planned for the near future. Was she a mind reader?

Charlotte smiled graciously and blushed again, but still didn't venture to answer. He couldn't let that make him feel daunted. If there was ever a time to go out on a limb for the woman he loved, it was now.

As things were winding down, and he'd said his final good-bye to Kiefer and Ashley and, of course, his parents and grandfather, he escorted Charlotte back to the car. He'd left his mother with some flabbergasting—to use her word—instructions, but she'd agreed to carry them out to the T, had even cried a little about it.

He also banked on Charlotte needing another good night's rest so he could finish planning.

Making his job easy, Charlotte was nearly

266   WEDDING DATE WITH THE ARMY DOC

asleep on her feet by the time they got back to the hotel. "Looks like you're ready to turn in."

"Sorry I'm such a drag!"

"No, you're not. You're carrying my baby. It zaps the energy out of a person."

"So you understand?"

"Believe me, I do. Plus Drew and Evan are going to meet me in the bar for a quick drink. I've almost got Drew convinced to come visit before summer is over."

"That's wonderful."

"Since I met you luck has been on my side and my life has taken a turn for better. You know that, right?" He hugged and kissed her long and hard, hoping his message had sunk in, then said good night. Before his sons arrived he needed to talk to the hotel staff to help him make those special arrangements for Sunday evening.

He'd asked Charlotte to marry him, she'd yet to say yes, but he still intended to tie the knot right in his own backyard. Hopefully before tomorrow was over, she'd come round.

He'd often heard that a wedding in Savannah was destined to last as long as the city's ancient oaks. That sounded about right to him. Good thing he'd shopped for her ring online at the best jeweler's in his hometown, in case she still needed proof about how he felt. He had it in his jacket pocket. Jarod had dropped it off last night, along with some expedited official paperwork.

Walking down the hotel hall toward the elevator, Jackson couldn't help but think he was wearing down Charlotte's resistance, so he grinned.

Charlotte had a great night's sleep filled with dreams of celebrations and dancing and happy faces. It made her miss her family, what was left of it. Her brother, Don, had made a career in the service and was rarely in California. Her sister, Cynthia, her husband and their three adorable kids, her nephews and niece, her baby's cousins. She missed them all.

It occurred to her it was time to phone both of them and break the news. She promised herself she'd do it as soon as she was back in LA. Maybe by then she'd have made up her mind what to do about Jackson and his proposal. She could imagine their jaws dropping when she announced, *I'm pregnant.*

Jackson was already up and whistling away in the bathroom while she was still yawning and trying to open her eyes. Where Jackson got all his energy Charlotte didn't have a clue. Usually dealing with estranged families drained a person, but he seemed focused and happy, and she hoped she had something to do with his good state of mind.

He popped his head around the corner from the bathroom. "I got tickets for us to tour the Mercer house this morning. I pointed it out to you yesterday when we were at Monterey Square, the place with the huge statue of General Pulaski?"

She knew exactly which square he meant, it had been her favorite, and she considered it the prettiest of the ones he'd taken her to. "Yes. The *Midnight in the Garden of Good and Evil* house?"

"Yes, that one, the Jim Williams story."

"Neat. I'd love to peek inside." Last night, when he'd said "So let's get married" she had been on the verge of saying yes. Every second they'd been together she'd felt her love for him growing stronger and stronger. Did it really matter that he wanted to marry her *because* she was pregnant?

"You feel like walking today? We can take the water taxi across the river and walk from there."

"After all the eating I've been doing, that sounds like a great plan." Fortunately, she'd worn comfortable shoes for the plane ride. When she'd finished with her morning routine Jackson was dressed and waiting for her.

"I'll make sure you're back in time for a nap this afternoon, too."

"Since our plane doesn't leave until midnight, that's probably a good idea. I'll have plenty of time to pack tonight before we leave."

"But I've made some special plans for dining tonight. Maybe you can pack this afternoon after that nap. I want you to be rested to enjoy our evening."

"Sounds romantic." And he'd probably want his answer then, too.

He took her hand. "If all goes as planned it will be," he said, guiding her out of the hotel room. "Oh, one more thing—you know how you said it was too bad you'd only get to wear that knock-out dress once?"

"Yes?"

"Wear it again tonight, okay?"

What did Jackson have planned? "Sure, if that's what you want." She didn't know why but chills rose the fine hair on her arms over his request.

Once downstairs they went out the waterside exit, passing the pool on the left and the pretty grassy area on the right. "Oh, it looks like they're setting up for a small wedding today," she said on the way to the water taxi.

"Well, they are famous for their wedding packages here."

"Looks charming." Only a handful of round tables were set up with white tablecloths, making a half circle around the small gazebo at the center. Someone had already draped cream-colored organza fabric at the entrance, and another employee was in the process of hanging crystal prisms on varying lengths of string, catching the light and casting rainbows everywhere. Maybe she should take notes and add them to all the mental notes she'd taken last night at Kiefer and Ashley's wedding.

Jackson was right, Savannah was a truly romantic city, and her old dream of having it all kept sneaking back into her heart.

A man of his word, Jackson made sure Charlotte was back at the hotel by mid-afternoon to pack and rest up before their special dinner plans. Later, as promised to make the man she loved happy, she put on the dress from yesterday's wedding, feeling just as elegant today.

She thought back to the day she'd bought it, the first time she'd noticed something different had been going on with her body, and the one purpose she'd had in mind while she'd searched for the perfect dress—to make herself a woman Jackson couldn't live without. Had she been successful? Maybe over dinner tonight she'd give him her answer.

Jackson had also put on the dressy suit he'd worn to the wedding yesterday, looking handsome as always, and very Southern. She'd noticed his speech had changed a little since coming back to his home state, sounding a little slower and warmer, and she really loved the Georgia accent.

She studied him. His brown wavy hair had got curlier in Savannah, just like hers had, and the light tan he'd picked up over the past two days made his bright blue eyes stand out even more. She wondered if their baby would get his classic nose or her own nondescript one. Or his shocking blue eyes. For no reason he smiled at her like he had a big secret, and the grooves on both sides of his cheeks highlighted that grin. Damn, he was sexy, and she suddenly had the need to tell him exactly what she was thinking.

"You are *so* good-looking."

He grinned. "And you, my lady, are a goddess." His eyes seemed to sparkle when he said the last word.

Well, that did it. They didn't have to leave the room, as far as she was concerned, because she'd been acutely aware that since they'd arrived in Georgia they hadn't made love. She might be pregnant and a little more tired than usual, but all he had to do was look into her eyes with those killer blues and touch her just so and, well, right about now she'd pretty much sign up for anything he had in mind. If he happened to whisper he loved her, she'd definitely give him her answer.

"So you want to get together?" she offered playfully and hopefully.

He took her into his arms and kissed her thoroughly, the kind of kiss that would require a reapplication of lipstick once they were done, and she started thinking they were definitely on the same page. But then he stopped kissing her. "Call me old-fashioned, but I'd kind of like to wait until after you decide if you want to marry me or not."

Was he blackmailing her by withholding sex? "Seriously?"

"A man's got to stand his ground for honor's sake." He winked.

Again, there was that secret worry that his proposal had been more about honor and not enough about love.

A minute later, with one last fluff of her hair and that reapplication of peach-colored lipstick, they left the hotel room just as the horn of another container ship blared its arrival and floated by their window.

"I'm gonna miss it here," she said.

"We'll make a point to come visit often, then."

She tossed him a look and got chills. He obviously wasn't backing down on his offer to marry her, making all these future plans and all. Maybe the guy really did love her for herself and not just because she was pregnant.

When they caught the elevator and ended up at the main floor, instead of heading for the five-star hotel restaurant, as she'd expected, he escorted her outside. She immediately remembered the small private setup on the golf-course-green grass near the gazebo and watched for it.

"Oh, look, isn't that just beautiful?" she said, wondering what the occasion was. Obviously it was a small and private affair.

"It sure is." He put his hand at the small of her back and guided her toward it.

She resisted him. "We can't crash someone else's party."

"Of course we can. Do you see anyone around? Let's just go and have a look."

Only because she was dying to see everything up close, especially now, since small clear glass vases of bright summer-colored gerberas had been placed at each perfectly set table, she agreed. "But isn't this taking nosy to a new level, at the expense of someone else's private affair?"

"I don't see it that way." Once they got close enough for her to see the fine hotel china and silverware, Jackson cleared his throat and raised his hand. "Can we get some help over here, please?" he said to a nearby waiter.

Her heart palpitated and her face flushed. "What are you doing?"

"Hold on, don't freak out."

The silver-haired server, wearing a white waistcoat, immediately snapped to attention. "Yes, Dr. Hilstead. Are we ready?"

"Just give me two minutes first, please."

Charlotte's heart went still as Jackson dropped to one knee and took her hand. With the other hand, he fished inside his jacket for the pocket and something small.

"I love you. I've been trying to prove it all weekend, and I hope you've caught on. Because I mean it. I'm a better man because of you, and I want to spend the rest of my life with you. I love you with all my heart, and I want us to be a family. Charlotte, since I met you I've discovered I'm full of love. There's room for my sons, and our sons or daughters, but most especially for you. Right at the center. Forever. Do you believe me yet?"

Her face crumpled. How had she not known his proposal had been sincere from the very start? He was a man of his word, but also a man of the heart. If he said he loved her, he meant it. "Yes. I believe you."

"Then will you marry me?"

"Yes."

Jackson's expression of joy promised to plant itself in her heart for life. "Thank God." He stood and kissed her, then flashed a beautiful ring as he gave some high sign. She could have sworn she heard muted applause.

"We'll hold the record for the world's shortest engagement." He slid the ring on her finger and she took a moment to admire the pure solitaire diamond's beauty.

With Jackson's affirmation and a snap of the head waiter's fingers, soft classical string music began to play the Pachelbel concerto, and a group of people came out from what seemed nowhere.

Now her heart thundered in her ears. She recognized Jackson's parents and grandfather—how could she ever forget him?—and both of Jackson's sons, plus a few other people she remembered to be relatives of his, one being his aunt Maggie. Nearly dizzy with wonder, she couldn't speak, even though her mouth was open.

A husky man around Jackson's age came toward them and Jackson introduced him to her. "This is my old college roommate, Jarod. Or Judge Campbell these days. He's a county judge, and he's managed to pull a few strings for us, and since we were here for a wedding, I thought why not make it two? Jarod's going to perform the ceremony. Are you ready?"

Her chest clamped down so hard she didn't think she could draw her next breath. Of course she wanted to marry Jackson, but right this moment? Right here? It was all his family and friends, and she didn't have anyone to represent her. She didn't want to spend one second ruining this moment with sadness, but the emptiness flicked her hard.

"He's going to marry us now?"

Jackson gave the most confident nod she'd ever seen. "Remember our saying? Life is all about what's happening right now. So what do you say? Let's get married."

"But I don't have anyone here, Jackson."

"We can get married again in California and you can invite the whole hospital if you want, but I can't wait another second to be your husband." His swoon-worthy words sank in and they seemed to be accompanied by the scent of magnolias. She was sure she'd never forget this singular moment when the man she loved asked her to be his wife. In front of a crowd!

"Actually," he said, "you do have someone here for you, and he's the perfect person to walk you down the aisle. All we have left to do is say *I do*. So if you'll excuse me, I'll just go stand up there..." he pointed to the decorated gazebo "...and wait for you." He smiled so reassuringly she couldn't think of a single reason to refuse tonight as the night to take her vows.

Doing as instructed, Charlotte turned to see Dr. Gordon standing at the back of the lawn, a sweet smile on his face, wearing a white summer tuxedo jacket and black slacks, and holding a small bouquet, which was apparently meant for her to carry. The head of the waitstaff walked her to him, and Jim Gordon proudly held out his elbow for her to clamp her arm onto. And, boy, did she need something to hold on to right now because Jackson had just knocked her for a loop! It seemed a lifetime of stored-up feelings had been unleashed as she took her place beside her mentor, and she'd never felt more alive in her life.

Her chin quivered and her eyes welled, and Jim gave her a fatherly, encouraging look. "Don't worry, I'll get you there, dear. It's time for your happily-ever-after. Now, on the count of three, follow me."

With that, she took his advice and dived into the moment, the what-was-happening-right-now part, and quickly remembered the special bridal walk from all the movies she'd watched growing up. *Step, together, step, together.* She thought about her mother and knew this would have made her ecstatic. And on wobbly legs, in front of a new family she couldn't wait to get to know better, she made her way to the gazebo, with the help of her mentor and stand-in father. There, the handsomest groom in the world, and the most perfect *imperfect* man she could never have dared to dream of, waited for her to say *I do.*

EPILOGUE

CHARLOTTE LOOKED UP at Jackson, holding her hand while she lay on the examination table. He smiled reassuringly and squeezed her hand.

"So at twenty weeks we do the official ultrasound. Are you ready?" the magenta-haired sonography tech said.

Charlotte studied the young woman's brow piercing while she considered the question. Was she ready? Now that she was married and she and Jackson were a team, any potential outcome of what they might find out about their baby seemed far less scary. "Yes," she said.

Jackson grabbed her hand again as the tech squeezed cold gel onto her stomach and began moving the transducer around her growing abdomen. Soon a pie-shaped section appeared on the screen and shortly after that a profile shot of their baby's head appeared. They gasped together in wonder. Charlotte's other hand flew to her mouth. Her baby looked perfectly formed with a cute upturned nose and a really big-looking head. Was there a thumb in the mouth?

"I'll snap that picture for you, if you'd like. Or maybe you'd rather wait in case we can identify the sex."

Charlotte's gaze jumped to Jackson's and he nodded, indicating, like they'd previously discussed, it was up to her. "I'd like *that* picture, please."

"Done." As the technician moved on, she described every part of the fetus's anatomy that came into view. "Depending on whether or not you want to know the sex, you may want to look away during this next portion." She held steady at the point she'd left off, waiting for Charlotte's reply.

Charlotte smiled contentedly, knowing without a doubt since she'd married Jackson that no matter what the sex of their baby, their love for each other and their future child would see them through any and all the challenges in life. Whether it involved DNA or not.

Right here and now she saw for herself that her baby was perfect in every way, growing as it should be. Jackson had been okay either way about knowing or not, so he kept quiet, just gazing benignly at Charlotte as she finally made up her mind.

He bent and kissed her forehead as she closed her eyes. Did she want to know the sex today? Would knowing add or detract from the wonder of her pregnancy? Since passing through the first trimester, she'd loved being pregnant. Feeling her body change and knowing something she and Jackson had created together grew inside her had put her in an incredibly happy place.

If there was ever a time to think of Dr. Gordon's recipe for living it was now. *Life wasn't about what might happen, it was about right here and now.* She had proof of a perfectly forming baby on the computer screen. Sonography didn't lie. Then she thought of her mother, because since the wedding she'd been doing that a lot. Her mom had once told her all about the day she'd been born. Back in the day they chose two names for every pregnancy. One for a boy and one for a girl. People gave generic gifts at showers, and the parents had the joy of discovering the baby's sex at birth. She'd loved hearing the story about the day she'd been born and how happy her mother had been that she'd had a girl.

Because she'd started to show, the women at work all seemed to want to share their own birthing stories, and one lab technician's stuck out in her mind. The ultrasound had indicated the baby was a girl, and they had only got girls' baby clothes and items at her shower. The problem was, she'd wound up delivering a boy! Her mother-in-law had had to return all the baby items and buy new ones, adding stress to the shock. They'd been expecting a girl and now had to adjust to having a boy. The ultrasound wasn't always one hundred percent accurate.

Charlotte turned to Jackson, his brows lifting as he waited for her decision.

"Let's do it the old-fashioned way and wait to find out when I deliver."

He laughed and clapped. "That's a great idea."

"Then look away," the technician said as she continued the test.

"You're peeking!" Charlotte teased Jackson, both of them giddy with excitement for their future as they stared at each other for the next few moments rather than watch the monitor.

"I'm not, I swear. You know I'll be happy with whatever we have…" he bent and kissed her, and she remembered why she hadn't doubted for one second how much he loved her since his amazing proposal in Savannah "…because whether it's a she or a he, our kid will make us a family."

Charlotte had lost the heart of her family way too early when her mother had died. Things had never been the same and when she searched her heart she realized that for years and years she'd longed for a family of her own. Until she'd met Jackson, she'd never dared to dream it could actually happen. "I like the sound of that."

"Our family?"

"Yes, *our* family."

* * * * *

*Look out for the other great story in
the* SUMMER BRIDES *duet*

*WHITE WEDDING FOR A SOUTHERN BELLE
by Susan Carlisle*

*And if you enjoyed this story, check out these
other great reads from Lynne Marshall*

A MOTHER FOR HIS ADOPTED SON

HOT-SHOT DOC, SECRET DAD

FATHER FOR HER NEWBORN BABY

*200 HARLEY STREET: AMERICAN SURGEON
IN LONDON*

All available now!

MILLS & BOON®
Large Print Medical

February

Seduced by the Sheikh Surgeon	Carol Marinelli
Challenging the Doctor Sheikh	Amalie Berlin
The Doctor She Always Dreamed Of	Wendy S. Marcus
The Nurse's Newborn Gift	Wendy S. Marcus
Tempting Nashville's Celebrity Doc	Amy Ruttan
Dr White's Baby Wish	Sue MacKay

March

A Daddy for Her Daughter	Tina Beckett
Reunited with His Runaway Bride	Robin Gianna
Rescued by Dr Rafe	Annie Claydon
Saved by the Single Dad	Annie Claydon
Sizzling Nights with Dr Off-Limits	Janice Lynn
Seven Nights with Her Ex	Louisa Heaton

April

Waking Up to Dr Gorgeous	Emily Forbes
Swept Away by the Seductive Stranger	Amy Andrews
One Kiss in Tokyo...	Scarlet Wilson
The Courage to Love Her Army Doc	Karin Baine
Reawakened by the Surgeon's Touch	Jennifer Taylor
Second Chance with Lord Branscombe	Joanna Neil

MILLS & BOON®
Large Print Medical

May

The Nurse's Christmas Gift	Tina Beckett
The Midwife's Pregnancy Miracle	Kate Hardy
Their First Family Christmas	Alison Roberts
The Nightshift Before Christmas	Annie O'Neil
It Started at Christmas...	Janice Lynn
Unwrapped by the Duke	Amy Ruttan

June

White Christmas for the Single Mum	Susanne Hampton
A Royal Baby for Christmas	Scarlet Wilson
Playboy on Her Christmas List	Carol Marinelli
The Army Doc's Baby Bombshell	Sue MacKay
The Doctor's Sleigh Bell Proposal	Susan Carlisle
Christmas with the Single Dad	Louisa Heaton

July

Falling for Her Wounded Hero	Marion Lennox
The Surgeon's Baby Surprise	Charlotte Hawkes
Santiago's Convenient Fiancée	Annie O'Neil
Alejandro's Sexy Secret	Amy Ruttan
The Doctor's Diamond Proposal	Annie Claydon
Weekend with the Best Man	Leah Martyn